Ghostly SNOW

GIRL AMONG WOLVES 3

USA TODAY BESTSELLING AUTHOR

LENA MAE HILL

Formatting by Lee Ching of Under Cover Designs

ISBN-13: 978-1-945780-49-3

1

For six months I roam the Three Valleys, killing every living being that crosses my path, messily and without ceremony or remorse. I crunch the bones of beasts large and small, from the tiny mouse to the fearsome stag. I am the most powerful creature alive, a white tiger in the green forests. On the hot days of summer, I burn inside my coat and spend afternoons lying on cool rocks in the shade, drinking from a cold, clear stream. In fall, I watch the wood smoke wind up from chimneys in the valleys, but I don't need a fire to keep me warm. In winter, when the trees have been stripped bare, I am thankful for the warmth of my thick fur.

Oblivious to the cold, I bound forward, the thrill of the chase humming through me like an electrical charge. The scent of blood draws me to it, this animal I have yet to set eyes upon. I leap from one boulder to the next, whip around the corner of a large one and through a passage between two others. Above me, a silvery bluff towers like a wall, one that even I can't scale. Neither can the creature I spot ahead, racing along the base of the bluff, fear surrounding it like a cloud. I gather my strength and leap for it, already tasting slippery, coppery blood in the back of my throat.

Knocking it to the ground beneath me, I roll it over

with my large white paws. But even as I am turning it, it is shifting and changing under me, transforming into something less animal than it was, than I am. Fur is sucked back through skin, bones snap and bulge, the skull flattens where it once was elongated. I open my mouth, showing it my sharp teeth and powerful jaws. The furless girl beneath me gibbers in a language I no longer understand, her eyes wide and terrified, her hair a wild tangle the color of autumn leaves. But I am an animal now, and I have no intention of going back to my weak and vulnerable human form to translate her words.

As if the thought has some strange power I don't understand, my body jerks suddenly, the familiar pull of my own limbs beginning to shift. I roar in protest, my head snapping back, my hips twisting painfully. I fall sideways, my skull striking the stone wall of the cliff. My prey scrambles away as I fight back the change, refusing to give in even as my own fur recedes into my skin, as my shoulders snap back. In seconds, my powerful body shrinks into something so fragile and helpless that a flimsy wooden door could trap it in captivity for three years.

My vision swims, distorting the trees into frightening shapes. Black petals blossom across my retinas like drops of blood on wet leaves. I have one moment of blind, helpless panic—*I can't go back into captivity*—before consciousness eludes me.

2

I wake naked and alone, curled in the leaves where I fell. I sit up stiffly, touch the painful lump on my head. What the hell? I reach for the tiger within, but she hunkers down, refusing to be coaxed from inside me.

Well, this is unfortunate. I haven't worn clothes in six months, hadn't known I'd ever need them again. It would be awkward to go home now, sneak into my mother's house—or my father's—to steal some clothes.

I reach for my tiger again, but she digs in further, sulking at the ill treatment she received. Maybe there is a limit to how long I can stay in one form. I didn't have time to learn much about being a shifter from my dad before I ran away. In truth, I probably know more about being a werewolf, like the rest of my family. For instance, I know they have to transition at the full moon, and if for some reason they don't for three months, they lose the ability forever. I've already spent six months without shifting.

Maybe it's like visiting another country, and you have to come back for a week every six months to maintain citizenship. Except I don't care about maintaining my human identity. I spent sixteen years as a human, and the last three have completely sucked.

Not knowing what else to do, I stand and start walking. It's too cold to stay human, with hair placed seemingly at random. It isn't very practical, this vulnerable human body. I mean, who needs fur under their arms? That's the last place that's going to get cold.

Suddenly, a vine whips around my ankles. I stumble, cursing my clumsy human body, and fall to all fours. Rocks bite painfully into my flesh and bones. Tigers never trip. And if they do, they sure don't go sprawling ungracefully in the dirt. Before I can recover myself, something falls over my back, something heavy and blanketing. I open my mouth to roar, but a girlish shriek comes out instead. As I push myself to my knees, panic churns in my gut, rushes in my ears. I'm in a net. Trapped.

God, I hate being human.

3

I must have tripped a snare when I caught my foot in the vine. Now the net lifts me, struggling and kicking, ten feet off the ground. I dangle in midair, swinging haphazardly until I tire myself out and stop moving. Curling into a ball, I shiver in the trap until it begins to rise. At last, it reaches the first branch of the tree. With a final heave, I'm yanked into the bare branches of the trees and deposited onto a platform. Soft tremors go through the tree as pairs of feet drop all around me from the branches above.

I struggle to free myself, but I'm still bound inside the net. Little creatures stand around me, poking me and uttering grunts and unintelligible words. I have seen a few of these things when hunting, in tiger form. There is something a few feet tall, with a flat face and a turned-up nose, the wrinkles in his skin lined with dust and grime.

A troll?

A smallish blonde creature with sharp ears, feathers in her long hair, and a pointy little chin, maybe an elf or a fairy?

Heavier footsteps approach, and the little creatures step closer to make room for the regular-sized human who leans over me. I bare my teeth at her and growl. "It's a feisty one," she says in a flat, nasally voice. I'm not sure if it's the girl I was hunting when she knocked me back into human form. It seems her hair is different, darker, but I see things differently through tiger eyes.

"What did you do to me?" I ask wriggling to get my hand through one of the holes in the net. "I'm a tiger. Let me go back."

A pair of worn leather boots lands soundlessly on the floor beside me, though the wearer doesn't so much as cause a tremor in the platform. "A tiger?" a voice asks. I twist around and find myself looking up at a small boy, maybe five feet tall, with delicate build and features. He leans over, his hands on his knees, and grins down at me. He has sharp, pointed teeth like a shark.

I shiver and draw my hand back into the net. "I'm sorry I was hunting you," I say, twisting around to see the human. Or whatever she is. Her hair is full of sticks and feathers, and one of those fox stoles with the head still attached lies draped across her shoulders. "I'll be more careful. I'm not trying to hurt anyone. Just let me go, and I'll leave you alone. All of you."

"And what are you going to do then? If we let you go?" She has a strange accent, maybe midwestern or northeastern.

"Nothing. I just want to be left alone. I'll go back to being a tiger, and I won't hunt any of you." I break off when the fox lying on her shoulders lifts its head. "Or your…animal," I finish lamely.

"If it idn't the tiger girl." She looks to the boy with the sharp teeth.

"Told you."

"You's right," she says, leaning in to poke me with one

6

sharp fingernail. "It's her, all right. What should we do with 'er?"

"Eat her for dinner," growls the troll.

"Can we keep her?" asks the elf, bouncing up and down and clapping her hands like she's asking for a puppy for Christmas. The platform shakes as if it might split apart under the sudden assault.

"Like for a pet?" the shark boy asks.

"She could be our familiar," says the elf.

"I got a familiar," the human says, patting the lazy fox on her shoulder.

"I think a tiger is my spirit animal," says a creature that could be the same species as the troll or elf, but looks a little different. She could be a dwarf or gnome. She has lovely black hair that's so glossy it seems to reflect every ray of light in the forest and a silky deep voice.

"Okay, let's keep 'er!" yells the human with the wild hair.

"Now wait just a minute," the boy says, leaning down to inspect me critically. "If she's the tiger that the wolf people have been looking for…"

"What?" I ask, trying to sit up, only to have the net yank me back down. The boy and the wild girl exchange glances.

"Can I please just get out of this cage, so I can hear what you have to say without being trapped in here like an animal? And stop talking about me like I'm not even here, if you don't mind."

"What if she runs away?" the troll asks when the girl steps forward to loosen the net.

"I'll catch her," she says nonchalantly. She digs a finger into one of the knots, flicks it open, and the whole net falls open. Now I'm completely exposed, suddenly aware of how very naked I am while everyone else is dressed. That's when I notice the boy isn't a kid. He's a tiny little man.

"Um. Thanks," I say. "You wouldn't happen to have a few clothes I could borrow?"

"Oh, sure," the girl says, grabbing a vine and yanking on it like she's ringing a huge bell. It wraps around her arm like a snake and lifts her off her feet. As she swings away on it, I glance suspiciously at the trees around us. The Enchanted Forest. Harmon said it was full of possessed trees and evil wraiths. They don't seem to mind the weird girl, though. A minute later, she swings back, and the vine deposits her onto the wooden platform, which is built on the branches of a large oak.

When I'm dressed in her clothes—a black skirt with patches of several different fabrics sewn on, a grey t-shirt and a brown fitted blazer worn soft with age—I turn back to the group. "I'm Stella," I say. "And yes, I'm the tiger that's been hunting here for the past six months. I hope I didn't eat any of your friends."

"Haven," the girl says, pressing a fist to her heart. "I'm a witch. I used to belong to the Winslow Coven, but I went rogue. So now I live here with all these other rejects." She gestures around with a broad grin, as if she's just given them a huge compliment. One of her canines sticks out at a cute angle making her look just a little cheeky.

"I prefer outcast, but yeah, basically," the blonde says. She's about as tall as my shoulder, with a sturdy body clad in leather boots, brown leggings, a green tunic, and a wide belt. She looks like a kid dressed up as Robin Hood, but when I study her face, I see that she's probably at least my age if not older. "I'm Xela, an outcast elf."

The guy with the sharp teeth introduces himself as Kale. He has fluffy bronze hair that feathers out around his ears, light brown skin, and warm, chocolate-brown eyes. He's only a few inches shorter than me, but his lovely face and delicate bones make him look smaller, almost like a doll. "Looking for my gossamer wings?" he asks with a smug smile when he catches me studying him. I take it he's a fairy.

The others introduce themselves in turn. The troll is named Yorn, and the girl with the shiny black hair is Uzula. She doesn't share her heritage, so I don't ask.

"So, what's your story?" Haven asks in that funny accent. "You an outcast tiger?"

"Something like that," I say. "Or I was, until you did your little spell. Can you please undo it?"

"Ah, now, you can't undo a spell," she says. "You'll just have to wait until it wears off."

"Great. How long is that?"

"Could be a few hours," she says, cocking her head and surveying me. "Could be a few weeks."

"Weeks?" I squeak. "What am I supposed to do? What will I eat? Where will I live?"

"I suppose you could live here with us," Kale says, smiling shyly at me. "Just until you're better. If you wanted."

"Quit flirting," Yorn grumbles, giving him a dark look.

"How can you not know?" I ask, turning to Haven. "What if it never wears off?"

9

She scratches her head, looking at the wooden floor. "Well, y'see, when I went rogue, I hadn't finished my training. So, I'm not really so good at magic. Don't blame me, I didn't do that to you."

"Oh," I say, relaxing a little. There's a long silence. "Do you know who did?"

"Nah, it could have been any witch. They live all around this valley, y'know."

Sinking to the nearest branch, I rest my head in my hands. What am I going to do? I never wanted to be human again. I gave up being human when I gave up Harmon. My human spirit is too fragile, my human body too breakable. A tiger doesn't think about how she had to choose between letting the one she loved turn his back on his people or stay and be the man that he was meant to be. A tiger doesn't wonder if the boy she loved will fulfill his destiny and lead his people to peace with all the other supernatural beings in the world. A tiger's heart doesn't break.

4

"I'm real sorry," Haven offers. "But you can, if you want. Stay with us. I got clothes you can borrow. You're not so much smaller than me. Those one's don't look half bad on ya."

"And we got warm beds," Xela says, sitting beside me and patting my shoulder awkwardly. "Real warm. And food."

"It would be a lot easier if I could hunt," I say, lifting my head.

"That would be so rad," Haven says with a big grin. "We'd eat like kings of the jungle." She looks a little bit crazy with that snaggle-tooth smile and her tangle of dark hair. But now that I look at her, I know she wasn't the girl who changed me. That girl had silky, pale auburn hair. And she was a shifter.

"Wait a minute," I say. "Whoever did this spell on me, she's a witch *and* a shifter. Is that possible? Or was she disguising herself as an animal with some kind of illusion?"

"Could be either," Haven says. "A witch is just a human with the ability to control the elements. Anything with a human side could be a witch, too."

I take all that in and then stand. All this supernatural stuff used to seem impossible, but now I just take it as it comes. "I might as well make the best of it while I'm here," I say. "At least I'm not naked anymore, and I'd probably freeze to death out there as a human. So…thank you. What can I do to help?"

"That's the spirit," Uzula says. "Let's show her the ropes. Then we'll have dinner with Doralice and tell stories."

Xela claps her hands together and jumps up and down again, shaking the tree around us with her sturdy little hops. "Someone new," she squeals. "We haven't gotten to tell anyone new our stories since…" She trails off and casts a guilty glance at Kale.

"Since Zinnia," he says, picking at a callous on his knuckle.

"Sorry," Xela mutters.

"Enough drama," Haven interrupts. "Let me show you to your quarters." With that, she reaches up again, and the vine drops down to snake around her arm. When I don't immediately leap at the idea, she motions impatiently.

I join her, gripping the vine. But when it starts to wind around my hand, I jerk back. "I'm not really…I'd rather hold on myself."

"Suit yourself," she says. "You'll have to hold onto me, then."

With that, she wraps her free arm around my waist and secures me against her. On her count, we do a little jump, and the vine swings us up. I'm not a big fan of flying. I'd prefer to keep my paws firmly on solid ground. But I have been known to lounge about in trees and take some questionable leaps from one high boulder to another. It's not much further than that. The vine swings us from the little platform up and over to the next tree. There, the vines don't seem to want to cooperate, so Haven sits down and has a chat with the tree while I try not stare at her like she's crazy.

"They're people like anyone else," she says when she catches my look. "Well, people and trees both, I suppose. If you're friendly to them, they'll be friendly to you."

I remember the juniper tree that scratched my neck and told me it was my mother. I remember the vine picking me up and swinging me against a tree trunk and knocking me out. "If you say so," I mutter. But I hold onto Haven as she swings on the relenting vine to the next tree.

"This is hot," she says, smiling down at me as I cling to her. "Maybe now's the time I should let you know that I'm rather fond of ladies as well as gents."

My face warms as the vine sets us down on a thick, arching branch of an oak tree. "Not a problem," I say. "I'm not really fond of either right now."

"Ah," she says. "That explains the murderous tiger."

She turns and lopes along the branch to a circular enclosure that looks like a hot air balloon turned upside down. "A lot of witches aren't choosy about little things like gender," she says. "All those people back there, they're my collective. That's what we call our circle of…what do shifters call it? Mates? Witches don't get just one mate. We get a collective of mutually beneficial relationships."

"Those are *all* your mates?"

"Yep," she says, hopping down into the balloon-like room. I find that after so long as a tiger, I'm wobbly as a human, but also fearless about walking along the branches and dropping into the swaying capsule with her. I wriggle through the opening and look around. It's about the size of a closet with walls made up of living branches of the host tree. I wonder if it's haunted, and if it gets mad, will it open the branches and drop me twenty feet above the ground or crush me like a Venus fly trap?

"Is this safe?" I ask.

Haven laughs. "This will be your nest. Everyone in the hive has one. That's what we call our little community."

"And...who all lives up here?"

"Right now, just me and my collective," she says. "We look out for each other, use our gifts to contribute."

"I'll find something to contribute," I say. "I can clean, build stuff... My cooking's edible."

"For now, just worry about staying out of the way of that she-wolf," she says. "Here's a hammock to sleep in." She pulls the item from a stub on the branch where it hangs and shows me how to string it up. "That's about it. We don't have much. We're the rag-tag crew of the Three Valleys. Like Robin Hood's merry men. Except we only steal by necessity," she adds with a wink.

"It's perfect. I really appreciate you taking me in like this. All of you."

"Sorry you had your magic bound up. Or whatever shifters call it."

"I'm not actually sure. But maybe you can work on undoing it?"

"No problem," she says. "Just warning you, though, it might make it worse. I might turn you into a mosquito. Shall I try now?"

"Um...maybe later."

Haven reaches up, and a branch thrusts itself into the hole at the top of the capsule. "Ready to go to dinner?"

As we swing back, I ask, "Am I taking someone's hammock? I could make up my own shelter if you have tools. I'm pretty handy with a hammer."

"No, that was Zinnia's. She came here with Kale, but she couldn't handle it, so she went back to live with the faeries. Broke poor Kale's heart. He's my newest addition. If you need to crawl in a warm hammock now and then, his is the one. I don't mind sharing a little."

My heart twists at the thought of moving on from Harmon, and I shake my head. "That's not necessary."

When we've descended from the trees, we follow a dirt path to a circle of stones. I glance around, my heart missing a beat. I've been here. I ran here once, when I was trying to escape the wolves. They attacked me in this very clearing, though Harmon tried to defend me. At the time, I thought it was my sister. Only later did I find out he'd risked everything, defying his father and Alpha, to protect me. I swallow hard and tear my eyes away from the spot where it must have been.

"Are we in wolf territory?" I ask, turning to Haven.

"Nah," she says. "But we're close. We hang out on the borders of the territories, where no one bothers us. If we tried to set up a colony in the valley, they'd chase us off. But no one's using this spot, so they leave us alone. Once in a while, someone will come up and cause trouble. But they're mostly harmless."

I keep my eye on the juniper tree standing at the edge of the clearing, though. I'm not sure it's harmless.

Yorn stomps around grumbling and shoving bits of

wood and dry leaves into the circle of stones at the center of the clearing while Kale skins a rabbit nearby. Haven snaps her fingers over the pile of sticks and leaves, and a spark flies from her fingers like she just hit two pieces of flint together. She catches me staring and grins. "Fire witch," she says with a shrug.

Once the fire is blazing, she takes me to a little stream and fills a black kettle, which she hangs over the fire when we get back. Uzula comes back from the woods with a handful of roots, which she and Xela take to the stream to wash and then chop with short, dull knives on a stone plate.

When the food is boiling in the pot, everyone sits along a fallen log next to the fire. I take a seat at the end, next to Xela, who begins combing her long, straight hair with a forked twig. "Who do you want to start us off?" she asks. "We have so many stories you haven't heard. What do you want to hear first?"

"Maybe we should let her tell her story first," Kale says. "None of us have heard that one."

"I don't think you really want to hear that," I say.

"Sure we do," Xela says. "You're an exiled tiger princess. Sounds exciting to me."

"It's pretty boring, actually."

"Tell us," Haven says. "How'd you end up an enemy of the wolf people?"

"Okay," I say, taking a deep breath. "I thought my dad died, and I came here to live with my mother. She kept me in her attic for a few years, so not much interesting happened then, except I found out about the werewolves. And I'm guessing you already know about them. And then

I found out my dad was actually still alive, and a shifter, so I went to live with him. But I guess you already know about shifters, too."

They all nod, and Yorn picks up a twig and runs it back and forth in the large gaps between his square teeth.

"That's why your mother wants to kill you?" Haven asks.

"I don't think she wants to kill me," I say. "But she's glad I'm gone."

They all exchange looks, and I get the feeling I'm missing something important. Haven goes to stir the pot of soup hanging over the fire. "Exactly how long were you in tiger form without seeing your wolf family?" she asks.

"Since last summer."

"What happened last summer?"

I quickly fill them in on my brief captivity with Harmon, and how I had to leave him so he could run his pack, and how my mother told me never to come back.

"There may have been a few changes since then," Haven says, picking up a stack of stone bowls. She ladles soup into them, and Kale passes them to everyone along the log. At last, they settle onto the log with us. "Of all the people in the Three Valleys, the wolf people are most secretive and isolationist," Kale explains. "The shifters, as you may know, have incorporated themselves into human society, while keeping their...alter identities a secret. But they send their kids to school and all that. And us...well, in this valley, there's the coven and a faerie troupe. Witches and faeries have a tense relationship. At one point, we were allies. But mostly, we inflict unspeakable cruelty on each other."

"Unspeakable," Haven agrees, nudging him with her elbow and giving him her cheeky smile. She lifts her bowl and slurps soup from it. Everyone else is doing the same. Since there's not a spoon in sight, I follow suit.

"All the other creatures live here, sometimes peacefully and sometimes not, but we make it work," Kale says. "Wolves are very territorial. They'll attack anyone who sets foot in their valley."

"I've noticed," I tell them.

"You hunted there as a tiger, though," Xela says with a belch. "Your Alpha is not happy."

"Our Alpha?" I ask, remembering Harmon the night I left. Does he hate me for that? I thought he'd understand, that he'd be grateful after the hurt wore off. I did the right thing.

Didn't I?

Haven wipes the back of her hand across her mouth. "She knows you're out here. She knows you come and go from her valley at your convenience, and she doesn't like it."

"She?" I ask, confused. "That can't be right."

"A-yup," Haven says, nodding grimly. "She's offering a reward for your capture."

I swallow hard and set my bowl on my knees, my stomach knotting. Is this a trap? Have they rendered me a helpless human, and now they're feeding me sleeping potions, planning to turn me in for some reward money? Yeah, I killed some deer and groundhogs and stuff. I didn't think that warranted a Wanted poster.

"Don't worry," Kale says, resting a slim hand on my forearm. "We're not going to turn you in."

"We could turn her in," Yorn grumbles. "Who knows what we could ask in return. Use of their land for gathering things we need, immunity from wolf attack…"

"Wolves don't attack here," Xela points out. "They never leave their valley."

"How about we turn you in?" Uzula asks Yorn, her black hair shimmering like a waterfall in the firelight. "You don't bring much to the group."

"We're not turning anyone in," Haven says. "We take in any manner of outcast, remember? All sins of the past are forgiven."

"Especially if they make great stories," Xela says with a grin. "Isn't that right, Doralice?" She looks up, and at first, I think she's talking to the sky. And then the juniper tree sways, and I freeze. I knew that name sounded familiar. That's what my mother called her, all those years ago. *Doralice.* My father's first wife. My stepmother. A freaking tree in the Enchanted Forest. And a friend of this band of oddballs who have taken me in.

5

When we've eaten, I offer to go wash the bowls in the stream, but Haven stops me. "You got a job to do first," she says.

I glance around, noticing the way the others are all watching me intently.

"A-yup," she says. "You've got to meet Doralice."

"I do?" I ask, swallowing hard. The tree stands sentinel over the clearing, looking as innocent as any other tree.

"You get to feed her," Haven says, placing a bowl in my hands. I hadn't noticed the extra bowl they'd left out to cool while we ate.

"Do I have to?" I whisper. "What if she doesn't like me?"

"Doralice likes everyone," Xela says. "She's just lonely. That's why we come up here to eat and tell stories, give her some company. And feed her."

"If you say so." I take a tentative step towards the tree. It stands motionless. Waiting.

It didn't hurt me before. It just grabbed me and didn't want to let go. It gave me a memory I didn't know I had and told me it was my mother.

I'm at the tree before I'm ready to repeat the creepy experience. It's so tied up with the wolf attack that I can't separate it. It seems ominous and dark, as dangerous as that night.

When I glance back, Xela motions me to go on. Kale gives me a sympathetic smile, which is a little more terrifying than encouraging, since his teeth look like they could slice off my hand in one bite. I kneel beneath the tree and set the bowl down. Someone clears her throat behind me.

Oh, right. Trees can't eat from bowls.

Carefully, I tip the soup out onto the ground at the base of the tree, though I wouldn't have minded having another bowl myself. Besides lacking salt, it was pretty tasty, and it seems a waste to dump it on the ground. I don't think trees actually eat anything but water and sunlight, but I don't want to offend the others by pointing out the silliness of their tradition. People have given sacrificial offerings for thousands of years. That's all this is.

Something scratches the back of my head and I almost scream. Instead, I hold myself very still while the spiny juniper needles rake over my scalp. "My daughter," her voice whispers into my head, as if it's coming from inside my mind instead of from the scratchy fingers in my hair. "You return to me at last."

I jerk away and scramble backwards on my hands and feet, out of her reach. Terror grips me as I remember those clinging branches that didn't want to let me go. Just one more thing that wants to trap me, imprison me.

The others are laughing. I jump to my feet, anger bubbling inside me. "What's so funny? Did you set me up?"

"Meeting Doralice for the first time is always an experience," Haven says. "What did she say?"

It strikes me then that they don't know. Of course they didn't set me up. They couldn't hear what she said to me. They don't know that she's my stepmother, that I've met her before. That my father married her.

I take in the faces of the others, amused and curious. No malicious intent. After living with my mother, it's hard to believe someone can laugh at me without it being spiteful or hateful. That someone might not have ulterior motives for each morsel of kindness dealt out. But I know better than to hope they might be a family to me. I've had two families—the father I grew up with, who was a selfish liar, and the mother who treated me like a disease. I'm not sure I want to tell the group what Doralice said, to tell them who I am to her. I don't know if I can trust them yet.

Taking a breath, I force a shaky laugh. "She spoke inside my head," I say.

"It's weird at first," Xela agrees. "But you get used to it. I like to sit on her branches and listen to her stories. And she likes us. She's a misfit like us."

I wonder how a tree can be a misfit, especially if there are lots of haunted trees out here. But I keep my mouth shut, not wanting to offend. Uzula comes down to the stream with me, and we wash out the dishes. My hands are numb with cold when we finish, and I hurry back to warm them by the fire when we're done. Xela goes to say goodnight to Doralice, and then we all tromp back through the woods to the hive. The night is cold and damp, and our breath makes little clouds in the deepening dusk. Leaves crunch underfoot, and I feel exposed and endangered in my human form.

"Want to sleep in one of our nests tonight?" Haven asks when we stop. It takes me a second to realize we're back at the hive already. If I wasn't looking up, searching for oddly rounded branches, I'd never notice the nests. I have to admire the camouflage.

"I'm okay," I say, remembering her invitation to climb in bed with Kale.

"It might be wise, just until the trees know you," she says. "They're not always hospitable to newcomers."

I glance around, my earlier ease gone. It was easy to feel safe while sitting around the fire with this lively bunch. Now that she's telling me the trees aren't so kind, I remember my mother's warning about the Enchanted Forest. I remember my own experiences.

"Once they know your intentions, you'll be fine," Haven says, squeezing my arm.

I pull back instinctively. "How long will that take?"

"Not long," she says. "Just give them a chance. Send out good vibes."

"Good vibes." I give her my best no-B.S. look.

"You'd be surprised what nature picks up on," she says. "Witches believe in energy. We harness the energy of the universe, of the elements. That's our magic. Don't be deceived by the apparent non-sentience of inanimate objects. You'd be surprised how much they channel your energy."

"Okay, sure," I say. "I should probably not trust the trees to carry me around until I actually believe that, though."

"You can stay with me. Don't worry, we'll grab your hammock on the way. Unless you'd rather stay in mine…" She wiggles her eyebrows at me.

"Thanks, but I'll be fine," I say. "I'm not interested in a relationship right now."

"Who said anything about a relationship?" she asks with a wicked grin. "You're not a wolf. Tigers don't mate for life."

I shrug, kicking at a mossy stone. "It feels like it right now."

"Too bad," she sings, skipping over to grab a vine. "Witches are rad lovers."

"I thought you had like five lovers already," I say, joining her. I wrap my arms around her and cling on while the vine lifts us up to the first platform.

"I'm a people person," she says. "And the others aren't all my lovers. I get something different from each of them."

"Ah. That's why you want to share Kale with me? Because he wants more than you're willing to give him?" Together, we swing towards the nests.

"Kale the person is like kale the vegetable. You know it would probably be really healthy and good for you to stick with it, but after a week, you just really want some chocolate."

I can't help but laugh.

We gather my hammock, which belonged to another girl who couldn't stick to her Kale diet and return to Haven's nest.

"Have you thought any more about whether you want

me to try to break your magic block?" Haven asks when we're ensconced in our hammocks in the dark.

I wish I had a fox to sleep beside me and keep me warm. Even with my hammock pulled tight around me, the chill evening makes me shiver. I should be out prowling the forest right now, hunting, warm inside my thick coat. The strangeness of the day catches up to me— being forced to shift and getting stuck that way, being captured and then befriended by a bunch of supernatural beings, talking to a tree who is also my dead ex-step-mother… Or whatever a father's secret ex-wife is called. Watching Haven snap her fingers and conjure fire.

I'm not especially anxious to have an amateur fire witch learn magic on me. "I'll give it a couple days," I say, shifting in my hammock. "Maybe it'll wear off."

"Have you tried shifting into something else?" she asks. "Maybe you're just blocked from your tiger form because, you know, you tried to eat a witch. Not saying you deserve it. But maybe she just blocked you from becoming an enormous deadly predator."

"What else would I be?"

"I don't know, a frog?"

I turn restlessly in my hammock. "Why would I want to be a frog?"

"Just to see if you can."

"I can't. I'm a tiger."

"Yeah, but you're not really. A werewolf is a wolf. You're a shifter, not a weretiger. You can shift into anything."

I go still at last. "I can?"

Haven laughs. "Of course you can."

"How do you know?" My eyes narrow in the dark. Maybe she was the one who attacked me after all. She knows a lot about shifters, and witches can disguise themselves…

"I've lived here all my life," she says, as if that explains everything.

"My father never told me that," I say, then realize how ridiculous that is. That's not even an argument. My father never told me a million things—that he was married before my mother, that my mother was alive, that she's a wolf and he's a mountain lion. That's what I thought he was. I didn't know he could be anything. That *I* could be.

Yet another lie, another thing about my true nature that everyone kept hidden from me. And to be told by a complete stranger makes the deception sting just a little bit more.

6

The next morning, I wake with a start. For a second, I fight the fabric over my face, sure I've been trapped. But then I remember where I am. I remember Haven telling me to zip my hammock closed to keep my warmth in before she fell asleep. For hours, I lay awake, unable to get comfortable in my human body, trying to shift into something else.

Now I hear a rustling sound in the leaves below our tree. I lie frozen, listening. I'm so helpless in my human form.

Maybe the spell only lasts for a day, I think hopefully. But when I try to shift, nothing happens. My tigress is fast asleep. I can feel her lurking there inside me, the killer instinct, the power and strength. She's alive, but she's not answering my call.

Slipping from my hammock, I catch my foot and fall against the wall. This human thing really sucks. I'm cold, I'm clumsy, I'm terrified of every little noise. It's probably just squirrels chasing each other around in the leaves.

Light filters in through the branches, and I shiver against the morning chill. Haven is gone, and the smell of wood smoke drifts up from somewhere nearby.

It's just your human side being paranoid, I tell myself. *Everything is fine.*

"We got another one," Yorn's droll voice calls.

Or not.

"Whoo-hoo," Xela cries. Her sturdy footsteps pound along a branch nearby.

Still wearing Haven's clothes from yesterday, I struggle up through the opening at the top of her little nest and nearly slide down the side and out of the tree. But just as I'm about to tumble twenty feet to the ground, a branch swings over and catches me. Before I can think, I'm laughing. It caught me. The tree caught me!

Now what?

I wrap my fingers around the branch, gripping it securely. Feeling like a complete idiot, I whisper, "Take me to the platform, please?"

Seconds later, it transfers me to another tree, and then another. At last a branch deposits me, still laughing and breathless with exhilaration, on the platform. I turn to find the others crowded around the net, where a struggling naked figure is trapped. My heart catches in my throat. Though he's moving too fast for me to see his face, fighting to break free, I instantly know who it is. Coppery tan skin, black hair. A tattoo on one shoulder.

"Let him out," I cry, my voice coming out high and desperate.

Harmon stops fighting and twists around towards me. I can't bear to meet his eyes.

"This one follow ya here?" Haven asks in her flat, accented voice. She steps forward, holding out one palm like she's ready to ward off an attack. With her other hands, she digs into the knot, and with a flick of her wrist, the net falls open.

The others take a step back when Harmon leaps to his feet, but he doesn't seem to see them. His eyes are fixed on me. For a long moment, no one speaks. Harmon's breath comes fast from the struggle, and his nostrils flare. But I can't tell if he's ready to kill me or kiss me. My eyes drop from his eerie, pale blue eyes to his lips, to his chest with the scars raking across it from where his father struck him when he defended me that night near the juniper.

"What are you doing here?" I whisper.

"Looking for you," he says, his eyes narrowing. "I didn't expect you to set traps. I thought you were a tiger."

"How did you find me?" I ask, ignoring the accusation and hurt in his voice.

"I tracked your scent."

"Well, it has been like six months since I took a shower…"

He doesn't respond to my attempt at humor. "I'd know your smell anywhere."

"Totally not weird," I mutter.

A glint of something flashes in his eyes, and his cheek twitches just the tiniest bit. "You're my mate, Stella. Nothing in the world smells better than your scent, even if you'd gone six years without showering."

"Awww," Xela says, clasping her hands together in front of her heart.

Harmon glances her way for the first time. She turns pink all the way to the tips of her pointy ears when he catches her ogling his body.

"Maybe we could go somewhere and talk privately?" Harmon asks, turning his attention back to me.

I bite back a laugh when Xela makes her hands into claws and mouths, "*Rawr*," behind his back.

"You can grab a skirt out of my nest if you need one," Haven pipes up. "I don't think you'd fit in anyone else's clothes. Unless, you know, you don't need clothes for this visit."

"Don't feel like you have to do it for us," Xela says. "We don't mind. Really."

Uzula slides her glossy black hair over her shoulder and gives Harmon a sultry look. "Yeah, most of us don't wear a stitch all summer."

Yorn stomps off down a branch to his nest, which sets everyone else laughing. He waves his hand dismissively without looking back.

"Aww, don't worry, you're still the handsomest man in the Three Valleys," Haven calls after him. I catch myself smiling with the others until I see Harmon's confused, wounded expression.

"I'll get you some clothes," I say, reaching for him. But I drop my hand before it meets his skin. What if he pulls back? What if he hates me? Worse, what if he did what I told him and met someone else? Maybe he needs me to release him from that mate thing.

We step over to the edge of the platform, and I reach for the vine. "You have to talk to them," I explain, feeling stupid even as I do it.

"Talk to the trees?" he asks, looking as distrustful as I did yesterday.

"I know," I say. "But it works. They warm up really quickly once they see you're not going to chop them down."

Harmon still looks doubtful, but he steps up beside me when I motion for him to join. I hadn't thought about how awkward it would be to travel with him this way. If it was awkward with Haven, a stranger, it's a hundred times worse with the boy who knows me better than anyone.

"So, just hold onto it with me, and we'll swing across," I say, trying to make my smile encouraging. If it scared me, and I'm used to being a tiger, it's going to totally freak out a wolf. But Harmon takes a breath and slides his arms around me. Instead of holding onto the vine together, as I did with Haven, Harmon holds all my weight and hangs onto the vine.

"What now?" he asks, looking down at me.

I try not to notice how warm he feels through the thin layer of my clothes. Try not to notice how naked he is, how tightly we're pressed together. So of course, that's all I can think about.

When I whisper to the vine, Harmon looks at me like I'm crazy. But his eyes widen when it swoops us off to another branch, which delivers us to Haven's nest. Inside, I throw Harmon a pair of pants and a long, loose skirt with an elastic waist. Though I saw him naked a hundred times when we were in captivity together, I turn my back while he changes.

"How do I look?" he asks after a minute. When I turn to look, he spreads his arms and gestures at the skirt, which stretches across his hips and ends just past his knees. It should be funny, but with his sculpted abs, chest and shoulders, it looks more like a man in a grass skirt or a kilt. A gorgeous man.

I swallow hard. "Hilarious."

Harmon smiles, though I can't bring my mouth to twist into that shape just now. Looking at him makes me want to weep, and scream, and tear the world apart for its unfairness. I'm a tiger, and he's a wolf. Shifters hate wolves, because wolves eat shifters. Only on occasion, when they don't know the animal is sometimes human, but still. It's happened before.

This feeling between us shouldn't be possible. It isn't natural. It's like that old saying, "they get along like cats and dogs." We shouldn't love each other. But I can't stop the throb of emotion in my heart when our eyes meet. Everything inside me crumbles, and I have to swallow back an ache in my throat.

A minute later, we're in the empty nest that Kale's companion left. "I guess this is me," I say, dropping down inside.

Harmon gives me a long, searching look. Then he steps forward, taking my face between his big hands, and kisses me. His mouth searches mine, pulling at me, hungering for me. It's the kiss of a dying man, hungry and frantic, full of pain and desire. His tongue slips between my lips, and my arms circle his neck. I crush his lips with mine, a bruising strength taking over my top half even as my legs go weak. Harmon holds me to him so tight I can barely breathe. But after only a minute, a second, not enough time to last me for six more months or even six more days, he breaks away and steps back.

Raking his hand through his thick, glossy hair, he turns away and rubs a hand over his face. When he turns back, his eyes are shiny, as if he's fighting back tears.

"You left me," he says, biting off each word as if just speaking them hurts.

"I had to," I say. "It was best for you. You know I'm right, or you would have come after me."

"You told me not to," he says, throwing his hands up. "You left without even saying goodbye. You told me you were going to be a tiger forever. And now I find you up here in the Enchanted Forest, living with a bunch of nudist elves and talking to trees. You could have told me when you changed your mind. When you decided to be human again."

"I didn't decide," I say. "I was forced to shift, and I'm still trying to shift back. I never wanted to be human again."

"But you are human, Stella," he says, sinking onto a twisted bulge in one branch that gives him just enough room to sit. "You're a shifter. Yes, you're part animal. Maybe half, maybe more or less. But you're also human. That's part of who you are, too."

"Yeah, well, I spent sixteen years as a human, not even knowing I had another option. Maybe after I spend sixteen as a tiger, I'll be ready to split my time evenly."

"Come on, Stella," he says. "I know you're mad that no one told you, but you can't be a tiger wandering free around Arkansas. Someone will see you. A human. Or are you going to go back to Oklahoma as a tiger, spend your life in a zoo?"

"You do it," I point out.

He looks at me hard. "One night a month."

I let my eyes slide away from his, over the contours of

his strong shoulders. "Did you do the other things I told you to do?"

He makes an incredulous sound and shakes his head. "You really don't understand how this whole Choosing thing works, do you?"

"You said until we had the ceremony…"

"…It wouldn't be recognized," he says. "I've still Chosen you. That doesn't go away. Never. Don't you get that? I don't want someone else. I can't. I never will."

"Oh." I look around for a place to sit, wishing I'd brought the hammock back from Haven's.

"That's what I came to talk to you about, actually," Harmon says, raking a hand through his hair again. He's cut it since I last saw him, when he'd been in a basement with me for months. I twist my fingers together, resisting the urge to reach out and touch that hair I love so much, to run my own fingers through it.

"You want me to come back?" The thought lodges in my throat, and I can barely squeeze the words out. I want to be with him again, to be his. But the werewolf community is full of people who despise and distrust me. And more than that, it's full of people I despise and distrust. It's full of memories of the past few years, of being a freak and an outcast and an unbearable burden. Full of betrayals and hurts and dashed hopes.

Which is why I left. I want Harmon, I've always wanted Harmon, but I don't want to go back there. And he belongs there.

"Of course I'd want you there if it was safe," he says, shaking his head. "But that's not why I came. I don't know how to tell you this, Stella. But your mother has gotten a little…crazy."

I roll my eyes and lean against the curving wall opposite him. "Tell me something new. She's always been a nightmare."

"She's gotten really strange," he says. "You know she took over when I was injured, right?"

"So I heard. And yes, I also heard that she wanted me dead."

Harmon winces. "When you left…I was healed. I should have taken over the next day. But your mother said that it was witchcraft, that you must be part witch."

I laugh at that. "Who knows? Maybe I am. I mean, I didn't know I was part tiger until this year. Hell, maybe I'm part troll, too. While we're at it, why don't we throw in that I'm a cannibalistic serial killer. My mother hates me, Harmon. She'd say anything."

"Yeah, well, she has," he says, not smiling at my joke. "She said that you bewitched me, not just to heal, but to Choose you."

The fight in me trickles away. "So…what does that mean? She had you Choose someone else? Elidi, right?"

"No, because I refused," he says, shaking his head and frowning down at his hands. "Which only made her more sure I was bewitched. And she's got half the pack believing it."

"But how? You're the Alpha."

"I was never confirmed by my father," he says. "He never passed on the gift to me."

"What's *the gift?*" My stomach knots, and I'm sure I don't really want an answer.

"To communicate with every pack member through the pack bond."

We sit in silence for a long minute. I remember my sisters telling me about this. It's what separates an Alpha from his second-in-command. It's what keeps wolves from defying their leader. They are compelled to do as he says. My mother may have control of them through her powers of persuasion, but she isn't their true Alpha.

But neither is Harmon.

"So how do you get the gift?" I ask. "There must be some way. Your father can't be the first Alpha who was killed before he passed the gift on to his successor."

"The Alpha is able to communicate because he needs to," Harmon says. "Which is always for the good of the pack and not himself. Talia is insisting that I'm not fit for Alpha because I'm bewitched. Otherwise, I would do what is good for the pack and marry someone from the pack."

A painful pressure burns behind my eyes. "Why don't you?" I whisper.

"I told you," Harmon explodes. "I want you, Stella. I couldn't Choose someone else even if I wanted to. And I don't." He strides across the small space in one step and sweeps me into his arms, crushing me to his chest. "You are my mate. My destiny." He strokes my tangled hair back and kisses me hard, desperately.

Right there, I decide that this is worth fighting for, even if it means the death of us both.

7

When at last he releases me, I sink back against the wall. "So, what does that mean? Are you leaving the pack?"

"No," he says, his eyes darkening. "They need me now more than ever. If this is my test, to prove I'm a worthy Alpha, then I'm not walking away from it."

"Can I help?" I ask. "What if I faked my own death? You could act like you'll be alone forever because your mate is dead. Mother couldn't say you were under my spell. And you wouldn't have to Choose someone else, if it's really as impossible as you say."

Harmon studies me and then shakes his head. "You don't have to do that. I'll convince them. I'll find some way."

"Convince them of what?"

"To get the gift without it passing from the former Alpha, the pack must unanimously pledge loyalty to the new Alpha with a blood sacrifice."

"What is that?" I ask, wrinkling my nose.

"It means they have to voluntarily submit to my bite," he growls, his eyebrows drawn low and his eyes thunderous.

"So, you have to convince every member of the pack that you'll be the best Alpha and put them first, and you have to do that by biting them?"

"Yes."

"Faking my death would be so much easier."

"I'd still have to get their loyalty," he says.

I shudder at the thought of him sinking his wolf fangs into everyone in the community. Yes, I've hunted and killed dozens if not hundreds of animals in the woods. But they were prey, not people.

"Yeah, but if my mother has them convinced you're going against the good of the pack, they won't voluntarily offer themselves up to be your chew toys," I point out. "Plus, she'll never submit. Once I'm dead, she'll have no reason not to. Everyone will see that she's just power-hungry, and they'll turn on her."

Harmon frowns down at his hands. "I'm worried about her," he says. "And your sisters, too. One day she'll be perfectly normal, and the next she's completely conniving. She wanders around the community at night, knocking on doors and getting people out of bed and having conversations with them like it's the middle of the afternoon and everything is perfectly normal."

"Welcome to the crazy-pants world of Talia," I say with a forced laugh. "If you ever say I'm turning into my mother, I'll turn into a tiger and literally bite your head off."

Harmon's head snaps up, and he gives me a triumphant smile. "So you are going to marry me."

"What? I never said that."

He grins and pushes himself up to standing. "I think you did."

"I'm pretty sure I didn't."

He stalks forward, slipping an arm around my waist

and pulling me against him. "I'm pretty sure you did," he growls into my ear, nuzzling his chin into my neck until shivers run all the way down my body and my fingers curl around his biceps. "I'm pretty sure you will."

"Are you?" I tease, tilting my head to give him access to my throat. "Hmm. Maybe. If you really beg."

His lips trail up the side of my neck. "Pretty, pretty please?" he whispers when he reaches my ear.

"I'll think about it."

He nips my earlobe, holding it gently between his teeth while he growls.

I giggle and push him away, but he pulls me back and smiles down at me. "Did anyone ever tell you that you're not very good at taking orders?"

"I seem to recall it being brought up a time or two."

"You know you can't challenge me in front of the others when I'm your Alpha. It'll make me look weak."

"Then I guess you better not order me around," I shoot back. "Because I'm not going to be your obedient little lapdog."

A hurt look flickers across his face. "I don't expect you to be."

"Maybe you don't mean to," I say. "But it's how your people work. Except you keep forgetting I'm not a wolf. Even if somehow they were okay with us being together after what I did to your father, will they be okay with me not being obedient to the Alpha? The exception to a rule everyone else has to follow?"

"I forgave you for my father," he says, smoothing my hair back. "They will, too. And I don't want you to be anything less than my equal." He cracks a smile. "But

39

don't be offended if I try to order you around. It's in my nature."

"And defying you is in mine," I say, smiling up at him. "So get used to it."

He kisses me tenderly. "I wish I could," he says when he pulls away. "But it's not safe for you back there yet. That's what I came to tell you. To warn you about your mother. She has it out for you."

"The others told me. She wants me dead."

Harmon cups my face between his hands and kisses me one more time. "She's angry, and she's got some of the others on her side. Saying you are responsible for what happened to their true Alpha. If I took you home, I'd be putting you in danger. I can't let that happen."

"I'll be fine as soon as I can shift back."

He frowns. "Then we'll have to make that happen. But you should stay out of our valley for now. I'm sorry. That doesn't mean I'm not thinking of you, missing you. Waiting for you."

"Harmon…"

"We're going to make it work," he says fiercely. "We'll find a way. We don't have another choice."

I don't remind him that we do. That maybe if he was mated with another wolf, it would be an unbreakable bond. My mother and father walked these footsteps before us. A shifter and a wolf. And they got divorced. My heart squeezes at the thought of leaving Harmon that way, forever fated to be loveless and alone, growing old and cold and bitter because he wasted his one chance at love on a shifty shifter.

I bring my fingers to his face, hold it between my

hands the way he's holding mine. "Okay," I whisper past the lump in my throat. "We'll find a way. I promise."

In this strange way, I suddenly understand my mother. I understand why she hates me. I'm the reason that her one true love, her forever-fated mate, had to leave. I'm the reason she's old and cold and bitter. And the thought of leaving Harmon that way breaks my heart in two. I could never do that to him. My father did that to my mother, and all I feel for her in this moment is pity. If she wants me dead, I can't really blame her. I'm the girl who tore her marriage apart, who broke her heart, broke the bond that should never have been broken.

Or maybe it should never have been made.

And here I am, repeating their story. Here I am, my father's daughter.

But I won't be the one to break Harmon's heart. Not again. I won't be the one to turn him cold, the decision he regrets for the rest of his life. He's giving me a chance, even after what I did. Leaving him didn't change his feelings for me at all. He's here, still protecting me, still warning me, still wanting me. And I still want him. Six months as a tiger didn't heal my broken heart. It only put it off. It didn't make me stop loving Harmon. As soon as I shifted back, it returned as strong as ever.

So did all the problems, though. Nothing has changed. Everything keeping us apart is still there. He's still not Alpha, and his pack still doesn't accept me. And I still can't make him choose between me and them.

"Let me help," I say. "Tell my mother I'm dead. You can work on getting the pack back on your side, trusting you. I'll stay up here, and she'll never know I'm alive. And when you're established as Alpha, I'll come back."

A frown darkens his expression. "I'm supposed to get my pack to trust me by lying to them? I'm not sure I like this idea."

"Well, I don't really like my mother putting a hit out on me. If she thinks I'm already dead, she'll call them off. I'll be safe, and you can take care of things there."

"Even if I told her, she wouldn't believe me."

"Bring her something," I say, looking around. If he brings my mother something of mine, something she knows I'd rather die than give up... Except I don't actually own a single thing. I gave Harmon my enchanted necklace, which is the closest thing I had to a meaningful object when I lived with my mother. Since then, well, it's not like tigers keep mementos. It occurs to me as I look around the little tree nest that I don't own a single thing on this earth. Even the funky skirt, t-shirt, and blazer I'm wearing belong to Haven.

"Bring her an animal heart," I say. "Tell her it's mine."

"Your mother knows I'd never kill you."

In desperation, I reach up and grab a pinch of hair at my scalp and rip it out. It hurts a lot worse than I was anticipating. Tears spring to my eyes, and I swear under my breath. Harmon looks at me like I'm nuts. "Bring her this," I say. "Tell her you found my body in the woods, and you had to keep a part of me, so you took a lock of hair."

Instead of telling me that's psycho, and kind of disgusting, Harmon takes the hair, as if my argument makes perfect sense. It probably does for someone who mates for life and can find his mate by her smell. Were-wolves love the drama. This is probably a perfectly normal and acceptable gesture for them.

"I'll try," he says. "If it means you'll be safe here until I get the pack under control." He kisses me again, this time passionately.

When he breaks the kiss at last, he presses his lips to my forehead. "Promise me you won't run away again?"

"Promise me you won't let my mother get away with this. This is your pack, Harmon. You deserve to lead it. That's your place, not hers." Squeezing his hipbones, I pull him in for one more kiss.

"I'll come and get you as soon as I'm pack leader."

I don't want to let him go. Now I remember why I left while he was sleeping. How can I watch him leave, not knowing if we'll ever be together? How did I gather the strength to leave him last time? It's all I can do to let him out of the nest, to swing back through the trees and drop to the ground with him. Every move is a step closer to goodbye.

I have to squeeze my hands into fists to keep them from clutching at him, begging him not to go. He can find a new pack, make a new one with me. He doesn't have to go back to those jerks. They don't deserve a leader as good as him, anyway. We could forget all of them, start over somewhere far from here where no one knows us.

But when I look at the white streak in his hair, remember the prophecy that says he will be the leader the pack is waiting for, I swallow back the protests. This is his place. He believes all this. This pack is his home, his destiny, and it has been since long before I came into his life. So I smile and blink back the tears that ache behind my eyes, and I tell him to return to his people.

When he leans in to kiss me again, I push him away. I can't take a long goodbye. I swallow the painful knot in my throat, laugh, and tell him to go, that I'll see him soon. After a hesitation, he peels off Haven's skirt and hands it back, then drops to the ground and transitions into his wolf form. He gives me a long look, his glacial-blue eyes inscrutable, and then turns and lopes down the mountain. I wait until he's gone to let the tears spill.

This time, he's the one leaving. If it hurt him even half this much, and he can still love me, then there's no way in hell I'm giving up on him.

8

I spend the next few hours fielding questions about Harmon and learning the ropes of the hive. The little group is welcoming, but I don't want to mooch off their generosity. During my time at Mother's I got pretty handy with tools and building, and I'm still strong from the work I did there and from all the exercise I got as a tiger. So I put myself to use as often as I can that day and over the coming days.

Even though I can't seem to shift into anything else, the group in the forest isn't a bad alternative. After a few weeks, I've settled in. Though I haven't stopped trying to shift back into my tiger form, I'm not a prisoner here, either. I hardly remember what to do with myself when I'm free. I've never been free before. First I had an over-bearing father, and then a psychotic mother. I've never had this kind of life, where I can make decisions for myself. Not until I found out who I really was. I can't help but wonder, if my father had let me know all along, if I could have been more independent.

Now I wait for someone to tell me what to do, but no one does. Haven says they all chip in, but as far as I can tell, there's not much to be done. They all go off into the woods each day. Apparently faeries are superb hunters, so Kale goes out to get food at least once a day. Yorn sets traps, and Uzula and Xela gather edibles in the woods. One day, I go along with them, confident that all the books I read in Mother's attic will finally pay off. Maybe I'll even be able to teach them something.

I'm sadly mistaken. By an hour into the day, even Xela has started to give short answers, sounding weary at my never-ending stream of questions. Turns out that without the book, I barely remember anything. If I had it with me, I could match the pictures to the plants, but I left that at Dad's with all my other things. Life was a lot easier when pretty much anything smaller than me was dinner.

After that day, I stay back at the camp. I don't want to risk being seen by a wolf or a wolf-friendly creature. Who knows how many people in the Three Valleys know about me. It's not like I was hiding, and white tigers aren't exactly native to the Ozark Mountains. Beyond that, they probably know that my mother is looking for me. After all, if even a band of outcasts knows, the people in the communities probably do, too. And some of them might be more tempted by a reward than Haven's collective, which doesn't seem to want anything from anyone.

I'm sitting in the clearing one day, making a wooden spoon with a pocket knife and a rounded stone for sanding, when a noise startles me. I straighten, my heart hammering as I listen for crackling leaves. It could be anything, a squirrel or armadillo, but it sounds bigger. The hairs along my arms stand up, and my tiger stirs inside me. She wants to come out, but she's trapped. Now that I'm free, she's stuck.

Carefully, I set down the wooden stick I've whittled

into a shape that's almost identifiable. I keep the pocket knife clutched in my hand.

Even though my tiger is trapped, I can sense the nearness of whatever it is, can sense it just beyond Doralice. I've started to come here more when the others are gone. At first, I felt silly, but now, I hardly notice that she doesn't answer. Somehow, just knowing that she was once human makes her more than a juniper tree. I haven't gone close enough for her to touch me again, though. There are limits to how human I can allow her to be before I question my own sanity. It's one thing to talk to a tree—back when I thought Dad was nothing but a nerdy botany professor, I heard him talk to plants plenty of times. It's an entirely different thing to think the trees are talking back. With all the fantastical things that have happened, I feel like I have to maintain a line somewhere.

Now I wait, holding my breath. I can feel the presence of someone there. I open my mouth to call Harmon, but I think better of it. Harmon knows where I am. He wouldn't sneak up like this.

I rise from fallen-log bench just as a figure steps into view. Sucking in a breath, I freeze. For so many months, I have avoided thinking about my mother. Even in the past two weeks, when I've been human again, I haven't wanted to do more than make bitter jokes to the other misfits about the evil queen. Seeing her again, in the flesh, brings a wave of fresh hurt that's so intense it feels like nausea. I want to throw my knife straight into her throat.

But I just stand there, my heart hammering, and do nothing. Just like I did all those days, all those years, when she threw me in her attic and withheld everything from me—my family, the chance at a normal life, and the truth. For a second, I'm that fourteen-year-old girl who arrived here knowing nothing, who wanted her mother's love and thought if she worked hard enough, she'd get it.

And then I'm not. My mother steps forward, swatting away Doralice's seeking needles, and the spell is broken. Whatever holds me taut in that moment snaps, and I remember who this is. That this isn't just the woman who locked me in her attic—chained me in her attic—but the woman who threw her own leader into a basement and told everyone he wasn't fit to lead because he loved me. After all, I'm so completely unlovable that my own mother hates me. Obviously, anyone who would dare to love me must need his head examined.

"Stella," she says, her mouth tightening into that so-familiar line. "You're alive. I knew it."

"I'm dead to you," I say. "And you're dead to me. Go away."

She looks around the dirt clearing with the small firepit, so meager compared to the large cleared space the wolves use for their gatherings, with grassy lawns, pavilions, and picnic tables, even a stage for their band to play. To her, our little squared-off stones and logs for sitting must look pathetic.

"I came to warn you," she says.

"I've already been warned," I say. "Warned about you. How did you even know where to find me?"

"A mother knows when her daughter is dead," she says. "I knew you weren't dead. And you weren't at your father's."

"You were never my mother," I say through clenched teeth.

She looks as if she'll speak, but then she stops and looks up at Doralice, standing over her. "This is the tree, is it? The ex-wife." Her lip curls at this word, as if it's something distasteful. I guess to a wolf, it is.

"What are you doing here?"

She sighs and steps further from Doralice, closer to me. And then, to my dismay, she smooths her long skirt against her bottom and sits down on a stone opposite the fire ring. I should throw the knife. But some part of me has to know why she's here. Did something happen to Harmon? To one of my sisters?

"I'll tell you why I'm here," she says. "And there's something you can tell me. It will be like before, when we traded information."

She gives me a smile that, to my horror, I think is supposed to be apologetic. Is she reminiscing about my time as her prisoner, as if we sat around making small talk?

What's your favorite food?

What's yours?

"I don't owe you anything," I snarl at her.

"No, I suppose you don't." She looks at me, her expression resigned, almost sad.

I glare back at her.

"How old are you, Stella?" she asks after a moment.

I glare at her another minute, but when she only regards me coolly, I have to answer.

"I wouldn't expect you to remember that about me, but surely you know how old your beloved Elidi is, and since she's my twin, even you can figure out that I'm seventeen."

"Do you know how old I am?"

"No, and I don't care."

"I'm thirty-three."

I don't want to care, but I do. I never knew that about my mother. I study her, the lines in her face, the callouses on her hands, the work boots on her feet. She looks much older, as old as my father or at least forty. She's younger than she looks, but it's no surprise I didn't know. How could I? No one told me anything true my whole life.

"So?"

"When I was your age, I already had twins to take care of," she says.

"Yeah, well, that was your bad decision," I say. "And if that's your excuse for being a shitty mom, it's not a very good one. I'm the one who paid for that decision, aren't I?"

She sighs and hooks her hands together around one knee. "I suppose I should have let her have your father," she says, looking up at Doralice.

"Why are you here?" I ask again.

"Your sister was the one who knew where to find you," she says. "Twin bond, or so she says. She knew you weren't dead. That's how I found you. That's what you wanted to know. Now it's your turn to answer."

"What?"

"That…woman. The mouse. The witch."

"Mrs. Nguyen."

She flinches. "Yes. She was just Yvonne when I knew her."

"What about her?" I ask, irritated that I can't simply tell her to go fall down a well. I actually want to know this stuff, why she's here, what led my father to marry her... After living my life in the dark, I'll take any light I can get, even from a fire that has burned me too many times to count.

"She's dangerous," my mother says. "You can't trust her."

Before I know what I'm doing, I'm laughing out loud. My mother, a woman who locked me away for over two years, here to warn me that the woman who got me out is dangerous. Mrs. Nguyen may not be everything she pretended to be all those years, but compared to my mother? I'll take my chances.

"You can't be serious," I say when I've recovered my senses. "If Mrs. Nguyen wanted to kill me, she'd have done it years ago. She was my babysitter for God's sake. I don't think she's out to get me."

"She's a witch," she says. "You can't trust a witch."

"Yeah, and I'm a shifty shifter, remember? Wolves don't trust anyone. And no offense, but compared to you, she's basically my witchy godmother. I'll take that over a jailer any day."

She rubs her temple, a gesture so familiar it twists something inside me. I hate that I know her mannerisms, that I know anything about her.

"I know that was hard on you," she says. "I'm sorry about that. I didn't know what else to do. I was always trying to protect you, Stella."

"Bull. Shit." I spit the words out, staring all my hatred at her.

"Of course you don't understand," she mutters. "You don't want to see my side of it, so you won't. But you should be careful of that woman. She's the true mirror. Do not trust her. That's all I came to tell you, when I found out you were staying in witch territory. It's the least I could do." She heaves herself up as if just standing exhausts her. "Watch out for yourself."

"Funny. Everyone else is telling me to watch out for you."

The corners of her mouth twist downwards as if she smells something bad. "I'm not here to hurt you. In fact, I'm going now." She holds up both hands as if in surrender, and it occurs to me that she doesn't know I can't shift. She thinks I'm sparing her out of kindness. I'm tempted to set her straight, but I think better of it. If she knew I was no threat to her, she'd probably have shifted into a wolf and ripped out my throat.

"Wait." I stand, moving toward her. I have the power of fear now, the same power she used over me so many times. For so long, I lived with the threat of what she could do to me. Now she can sweat a little. "Is Harmon okay?"

"He's fine," she says, her chin rising. "I'd not hurt my own pack members."

"Just your daughter," I say. "But I guess that doesn't count, since I'm not a wolf."

"I didn't have to come here," she says. "I didn't have to warn you."

"You shouldn't have bothered," I say. "I don't believe a word you say."

"You should," she says. "That witchcraft she does—

projection. It's more dangerous than you know. I hope this one time, you'll listen when I tell you what's good for you."

"Oh, that's rich," I say, balling my hands into fists. I want to slap her like she slapped me all those times. I want to knock her to the ground, make her shake with fear. "Like you kept me locked up for my own good? Like you lied to me for my own good?"

She draws herself up to her full height and looks down at me in that way that makes me feel like a small, spoiled child. "Goodbye, Stella."

I don't know why I let her get to me, why I let her make me feel anything, for even a moment. But I'm so angry.

"Hey," I bark, striding forward to grab her shoulder. "You don't get to walk away this time." When she turns, I have to fight the urge to shrink back from her burning eyes. I'm no longer that girl who cowered on the floor when she hit me.

"Is that so?" she asks with that haughty tilt to her chin.

Rage blooms inside me. I'm the one who can hurt her now. I'm the bigger animal. And yet, she still treats me like I'm nothing but a human nuisance. Before I know what I'm doing, my hand is whipping through the air, across her cheek.

9

Stunned, I step back, releasing her shoulder, starting to apologize even as my hand stings from the blow.

My mother doesn't wait for the apology. She grabs my shoulders and throws me to the ground. The packed dirt knocks the breath from me as I fall flat on my back. I scramble to get up, but my mother leaps onto me, still young enough to be nimble and a hell of a lot stronger than me. Where is my damn tiger when I need her?

Mother's hand blazes across one cheek and then the other. "Don't you ever disrespect me like that," she snarls, her eyes flashing.

To my utter humiliation, tears spring to my eyes. But my mother isn't looking at me. Her eyes fix on something beyond me, across the clearing. At first, I think it must be Doralice, but she's off to our right. Before I can twist around to see what's gotten her attention, she's knocked ten feet across the clearing, tumbling to a stop beneath Doralice.

Kale crouches over me, his tiny, needle-sharp teeth still bared. He quickly draws his lips down to cover them, grabs my hand, and pulls me to my feet as if I weigh nothing. I'm used to his faerie agility—he rarely uses the vines to move through the trees, but leaps from one to another like he belongs to some other realm of suspended animation—but I've never stopped to think how much strength that must take.

"Are you all right?" Kale asks, his brow furrowing.

I quickly swipe the tears from my cheeks, the humiliation of letting them show smarting worse than my cheeks. Across the clearing, my mother shrieks like she's been impaled. My stomach lurches. But when I turn to her, she's not being shot with a thousand needles from the juniper or dismembered by the vengeful branches of my father's first wife. She's crouched on one knee, her head in her hands. For a second, I think she's crying, too. But then she stands, lunges for Doralice, and twists one of her branches until it snaps.

Kale winces, but he doesn't leave my side. My mother falls to all fours this time, her body wracked with something that looks like a sob. I can't be sure, though, because she transitions into a wolf form and races off into the woods, leaving her skirt and boots behind. Her plaid shirt hangs awkwardly from her wolf shoulders as she slips through the trees and disappears down the mountain.

The sound of thudding feet pulls my attention back to the clearing, where Uzula and Xela have emerged from the trail, faces flushed and eyes wide. "What happened?" Xela asks.

"Nothing," I mutter, glancing at Kale.

He frowns but doesn't contradict me.

"Oh, Doralice," Uzula says, rushing over to peer at the broken branch. Despite running through the woods, her hair hangs as silky and shiny as ever, not a strand out of place. She turns accusing eyes on me. "Did you break her?"

I swallow hard. If I deny it, I'll have to tell them about my mother.

"It wasn't her," Kale says quickly. "It was…a werewolf." He nods to the abandoned skirt and boots lying at the foot of the juniper.

"Oh, you poor dear," Uzula says to the tree, turning back to examine the raw, jagged wood showing through the break. The rest of the branch still hangs on below the break. For a second, I think she might actually straighten the branch and bandage it.

But then Haven comes skipping into the clearing, her fox on her heels. "Ooh, boots," she says, picking up one of my mother's abandoned work boots. Yorn comes clomping up a minute later looking even grumpier than usual, with a groundhog hanging from his short, thick hand. Everyone keeps asking what happened, so finally, I sit down and give them an abbreviated version. They all sit around listening, except Uzula, who is still fretting over Doralice.

"Maybe you should stay up in the trees while we're out," Haven suggests later, when we're all seated along our log, eating meat from our bowls.

"I spent years trapped in her attic," I say slowly. "I'm not really keen to be trapped in the trees because of her."

"You wouldn't be trapped," Haven says. "And you could still come down and be with us when we're here. But maybe, just until you're shifting again, it wouldn't hurt to be cautious."

"You don't have to stay up there all day," Kale says. "You could climb up if you heard someone coming."

I frown into my bowl and set it on the ground at my

feet. "I can't keep running from her forever. Letting her control me through fear is letting her win."

"There's being brave, and there's being stupid," Yorn says, not looking up from the bone he's gnawing.

"We just don't want you getting hurt," Kale says quietly. His dark eyes are so intense I feel my face warming.

"Yeah, we've gotten kind of used to your singing," Haven says. "It brightens up the place."

"I don't sing," I say, my face getting even hotter.

"You're always singing," Yorn grumbles.

I am? I mean, sometimes I hum when I'm building something. I did that at Mother's, so I'd have something besides silence. When the mice weren't around, it seemed preferable to talking to myself.

"It's not terrible," Uzula assures me. "You're no song-bird, but no one's eardrums have exploded yet."

"And your cooking's not bad," Xela says. "Less gritty than ours."

"I don't miss the sand in my soup," Yorn grudgingly agrees.

"The spoons are a nice addition," Kale says.

"They make me feel so civilized," Xela says.

"I could do without all that," Yorn says. "Just one more thing to wash."

"Okay, okay, I'll stay at the nests," I say. "If anyone comes, I'll climb up into the trees and hide. Everyone happy with that?"

I pick up my bowl to finish my food, only to find it empty. When I turn around, Haven's fox is sitting a few feet behind the bench, licking his lips. His pointy little nose seems to twitch, his eyes gleaming with triumph.

After spending years thinking of animals as terrifying, and then months thinking of them as food, it's hard to get used to having a pet around. When I had mice, they always waited for their crumbs. I shake my head at the fox, but I know better than to scold it. It's not just a pet to Haven. It's part of her magic, somehow.

I take the bowls and head for the stream. A minute later, I hear footsteps behind me and stand, on alert. Kale steps from the trees holding the black cooking pot and some wooden utensils.

I relax and turn back to the stream. "I'm sorry about earlier," Kale says, crouching beside me and scooping up water with the pot. "If you didn't want me to say anything."

"No, it's fine," I say. "Thank you for…helping with my mother."

For a minute, we wash in silence. My mind moves back to a time I washed dishes beside Harmon, when he was still a stranger to me. The day of my first kiss.

Suddenly, the silence with Kale feels stifling, awkward. "You didn't have to come down here," I tell him, plunging a bowl into the icy water. "I don't need a bodyguard."

"I know," he says, looking wounded.

"I just meant, I'd feel like a burden if I had to be escorted everywhere. But thank you for coming down to make sure I'm okay."

"Just helping wash the dishes," he says, his attention riveted on a wooden spoon I carved. We finish washing the bowls and spoons in silence. When we're done, he holds out the pot, and I stack the bowls inside, acutely aware of his warmth every time my frigid hands brush against his. In silence, we make our way back to the clearing, only to find it empty. Everyone has gone to their nests, leaving only a few coals glowing in the fire pit.

"Don't worry," Kale says as we step onto the dark path leading to the hive. "I'll keep you safe."

I cut my eyes sideways at him, but I don't say anything. All I want to do is run away from this, all the way back down the mountain and back to Harmon, where I belong. Except I don't belong there. I don't belong anywhere, which lets me belong with these misfits.

Back at the hive, I stop and wait for a branch to take me up. But this time, Kale slips an arm around my waist and, before I can protest, leaps into the tree. I stifle a cry of surprise. Kale sets me down on the platform, and I catch the glint of his sharp teeth as he smiles. "If you wanted," he says slowly. "If you don't feel safe…"

"I do," I say quickly. "I feel safe. Thanks for the lift." Then, before things can get even more awkward, I head to my own nest. Inside, I zip myself into my hammock and lie there, waiting. I'm not sure what I'm waiting for, but I can't sleep. Somewhere nearby, a couple of the others are still talking in low voices. After a long while, when the voices have fallen silent, I slip out of my nest. The night is bitter, and my breath makes plumes of white in the dry air. I creep along a branch, illuminated by the rising moon.

When I reach the familiar nest, I hop up and slip through the opening in the branches. Haven's hammock hangs slack like a deflated balloon. For a minute, I stand there staring at it stupidly. But then I climb out and tiptoe back along the branches, trying not to notice that Kale's nest is rocking steadily. I slip back into my own nest and into my hammock, feeling guilty, as if I spied on them. But I'm also painfully lonely as I nestle down into my hammock and try to sleep.

Not that I wanted to be with either of them, not in that way. I just wanted a friend to tell these things to, a friend like I haven't had in years. But I guess Kale didn't mean much by his invitation. Like Haven said on my first night here, he's lonely. And all these misfits, they have each other. They have cut ties with their people. They can move fluidly from one nest to another. And although I fit in with them, my heart is somewhere else. I don't know how to get it back or even how to want it back.

10

For a while, I stay close to the hive during the day. But it gets boring. I find myself actually missing life with my mother, when I had ready access to any tool I could wish for. If she didn't have one, she'd borrow it from someone in the community, and within a day, I'd have it. Here, I'm surrounded by trees, by wood, but I have nothing to build with. And I have a feeling the trees might not be so friendly if I started cutting and plaining them to make furniture.

After a few weeks, I start to wander. I'm careful not to wander down the side of the mountain into the wolves' valley. But when I go the other way, I stumble upon an old rock wall one day, no more than a foot high and halfway buried in leaves. It's the kind of old-fashioned wall that is nothing more than a snaking line of stones piled up to mark the boundary. Nothing solid holds the stones in place. I step over the wall and catch sight of something I haven't seen in a long while—the white lookout tower I spotted long ago.

I head toward it, not having anything else to do. When I reach the tower, I'm out of breath, my lungs aching with the cold winter air. The whiteness of it nearly blinds me as I step out from behind the trees. The tower stands in a small clearing, choked with thick, tan grass and tangles of skeletal briars. I have to crane my head back to look up at it, at the lone window near the top, beneath the red shingles of the roof. It's a strange lookout tower, without an observation deck. More than ever, it resembles an old lighthouse.

There's no door on this side, but curiosity gets the better of me. I wade across the field, brambles ripping at my ragged skirt, a hand-me-down from Haven. I'm halfway there when I sense someone's presence. My head swings around, and I scent the air before I catch myself doing it. Stepping up to the tower, I flatten my back against it and wait, holding my breath. The wall is rough behind me, with tiny cracks running through the thick layer of white paint. It obviously has not been painted in a long time—dirt and pollen and a layer of fine, dead algae cling to the walls. And under my hands, something sharp. When I look down, impossibly, it looks like tiny barnacles cling to it. Surely it can't have come from the ocean. Why is a lighthouse in the middle of the landlocked mountains?

Before I can ponder it further, a girl steps around the side of it, into my view. She has shiny, light auburn hair piled into an impossible stack on her head, like some kind of beehive hairdo from the 1960s. I recognize her instantly. Like the last time I saw her, she's completely naked, despite the cold. Oblivious to my presence, she skips along until she's right beside me.

When she notices me, she shrieks, her hands flying to her mouth. A handful of hickory nuts falls from her hand and scatters across the ground at her feet. Without a word, she turns and dashes away, the nuts rolling under her feet as she goes. Recovering from my surprise, I spring after her.

She's fast, racing along the curve of the lighthouse, her bare feet seemingly accustomed to the jagged concrete ledge that runs around the base. I race after her, turning my ankle when I step on the edge of the ledge, which is about a foot wide and an inch above the dirt, as if it were ripped up with the lighthouse and transplanted here instead of built here, like a foundation would be.

I curse under my breath and step away from the wall, where I can run on the grass and dirt. Unlike her, I don't have to worry about the thorns, since I'm wearing my mother's boots.

"Wait," I call after her. "I need to talk to you."

I'm sure that at any moment, she's going to reach the door and disappear inside. Instead, she begins to wave her arms, and a second later, the air bursts into a flurry of motion. I throw up my hands to shield my face from the swirling wind and dust. Through my fingers, I see a golden eagle flapping its wings, rising up and around the wall of the tower. The girl is gone.

I sink against the side of the lighthouse, wanting to scream in frustration. But I'm also in awe. I've seen my father shift, and I know that shifters transition much more smoothly than wolves. But I've never seen someone shift like that, in mid-stride. I curse myself for being taken by surprise. I lost my chance to catch the girl who put this curse on me, forced me to be human again.

Stepping back from the tower, I look up. The eagle has disappeared, but I don't see it anywhere in the sky. It must have flown in through the window of the lighthouse.

"Hey," I call. "I'm not going to hurt you. I just want to talk."

The only answer is the wind rattling through the bare trees, rustling the leaves on the ground.

"You forgot your nuts," I try.

Nothing.

With a sigh, I turn and trudge back across the clearing. When I look back at the lighthouse, I'm sure I see a shadow moving in the window. But when I call back again, there's no answer, no movement.

"I just want to be able to shift back," I yell at the tower. "I won't hunt you. Please help me. Please?"

Nothing.

Defeated, I hurry back to the hive so no one will worry. I'm not supposed to wander so far. But every few steps, I turn and look over my shoulder, scanning the sky for a golden eagle. The sky remains a piercing, clear blue without a bird in sight.

A few days later, as we're sitting along the log at dinner, huddled close together against the bitter wind, I wait for a lull in the conversation.

"What's up with that tower?" I ask. "Arkansas seems like a strange place for a lighthouse."

"You don't know about the lighthouse?" Xela asks, turning to me with wide, excited eyes.

"No," I say through gritted teeth. I hate how everyone knows everything, and I'm always in the dark.

"They say the sorceress brought it," Haven says in a hushed tone. "When she came here from the sea."

"The sorceress?"

"Yes," Haven says. "She lives with the witches, but she's not really a witch. She says she was gifted the magic of a Winslow Witch, so now she's one of them. But people say she stole the magic."

"You can steal magic?"

"Some people can," she says with a nod. "But it's obviously a major crime for a witch to steal another's magic. She's not a natural witch, because she didn't have elemental powers. She has other powers."

"Like what?" I ask, remembering the girl who knocked me back into human form.

"Lots of things," Haven says. "No one knows for sure everything she can do. But witches are usually content to just do their magic and keep to themselves. They self-govern. She's obsessed with power, and beauty, and all the things true witches don't care about."

"What does she look like?" I ask, narrowing my eyes. I see that stack of auburn hair, the glowing skin, the vague sense of familiarity. Definitely beautiful.

"Who knows?" Haven says with a shrug. "She wears many faces. That's what they say."

I remember the revulsion the wolves felt for me, because I am an identical twin, as if that meant I was a *mirror*, their name for a person who steals another person's body. Maybe a person who wears many faces does the same. Or maybe she does illusion spells.

"Have you ever seen her?" I ask. "Does she live in that tower?"

"No one can live there," Kale says. "There's no door. You can't get in or out."

I remember the bird flying in the window high above the ground. Someone can get in and out.

I chase a tiny yam around my bowl with one of the wooden spoons I made before I ask the next question. "Is she also a shifter?"

"Not that I know of," Haven says. "But who really knows for sure? I've heard she can take the form of an animal, but she kills it in the process."

My heart thumps hard in my chest. "Projecting?"

Haven shudders and nods, and Xela looks at her bowl like she's just lost her appetite. Even Yorn scrunches down on the log with a gloomy expression on his face. Now would probably not be a good time to tell them I'm supposedly able to do this, too.

I have to force the next words out. "Do you think she's the one who…did this to me?"

Haven tilts her head and squints at me. "I thought you said she was a shifter?"

"She definitely shifted," I say, remembering the way she shifted in mid-stride, in a burst of flapping wings and dust.

"Then it's not the sorceress," Kale says with a reassuring smile.

"As far as we know," Haven adds.

"Could a witch block me from turning back into a tiger? That's not elemental, right?"

"Anyone can bind magic," Haven says. "Well, any witch."

I sigh and stand to collect the bowls. I'm no closer to finding out who she was than before I asked. As Haven and I walk to the stream to wash up, I find more questions spinning through my mind. "You're sure no one lives in that lighthouse?" I ask. "Why else would the sorceress bring it here?"

"I'm not really up to speed on all the witchy history," she admits, holding out her palm and making a tiny glowing fireball to light our way through the darkness. "But I know you can't get into the lighthouse. It's not like witches really fly on broomsticks. If you were going up there, you'd need a really tall ladder, that's for sure."

But she's thinking like a witch, and the others think like what they are. I'm a shifter, so I'm thinking like a shifter. And any shifter who could turn into a bird could fly up there, no broomstick required.

"So no one knows what this sorceress looks like or where she lives?" I ask as we crunch through the frost-edged leaves underfoot.

"She lives in the First Valley," Haven says, crouching beside the stream. The light blinks out when she plunges her hands into the icy water. "She's part of the coven."

I think I know the answer to the next question before I ask, but I have to know. My stomach knots, but I swallow the sour taste in my mouth and force the words out. "What's her name?"

"Yvonne."

I thought I was prepared for the answer, but it still makes my guts twist. Yvonne, my childhood neighbor and babysitter, the mouse who kept me company and probably saved my sanity during my time in the attic. How can I tell these people I'm friends with someone they see as a dangerous, dark sorceress?

I decide to keep my mouth shut for now. She's no threat to them, and she's not out to get me. As far as I can tell, she's just another person with a magic they don't understand, so they call her dangerous. The same way the wolves did to me, because I was an outsider, an *other*. Even more frustrating, I still don't know who the girl in the lighthouse is, why she blocked my ability to shift, and how I can get it back.

11

For the next week, I sneak away to the lighthouse every day. I walk around it, exploring the curved walls with their layers of white paint as thick as a dime. I approach through the field grown up with weeds, but when I circle the entire building, I see that one side is right at the edge of the slope of the mountain. From the top, you could probably see out for miles, over the entire valley—maybe all three valleys of supernaturals.

Turning back to the wall, I tap on it with my knuckles. It's solid as stone. I continue around the side and find a tangle of vines growing up the bottom part of the wall, broken midway up so they fall back in defeat, creating a giant mess to climb over. Since making friends with the trees so quickly, I'm not as wary of the vines in the forest, but I'm not sure about these. What if the sorceress grew them, and they are full of malice? But then I shake my head at the thought. The sorceress is Mrs. Nguyen—cat lady, mint-eater, daytime television watcher.

I begin to climb over the tangle of vines. Some snap under my weight, but none grab me. As I pass a thick cord of them, I see why. They've been cut across the base, killing the vines. I make it across and scramble up the slope to the field again, brushing off bits of bark from the vines that stick to my misshapen sweater and patchwork pants. When I see a figure in the field, I freeze.

For a second, she doesn't see me, and my mind races through possibilities. Mrs. Nguyen? The auburn-haired girl? But no, she's too big and solid to be that waif of a shifter. She's crouched low, as if digging in the ground, with her back to me. After a minute, she stands, and I suck in a breath.

"What are you doing here?" I demand, as if this mountain belongs to me.

My mother startles, then fumbles to keep from dropping the basket that hangs over her arm. "Stella," she says, then forces a high, false laugh. "I hardly recognized you. You scared me."

"I should," I say, stepping towards her. "You're way out of your valley, Mother. And you're not a true Alpha, so you can't communicate with your pack, can you?"

"You wouldn't hurt me," she says, but her voice sounds less sure than usual, almost tremulous.

Power surges through my chest. "Of course not," I say, stalking closer. "Just like you'd never hurt me, right? Since you're my mother and all."

"That's right," she says, squaring her shoulders. Instead of her usual drab flannels, she's wearing a long-sleeved tee with a velvet capelet and black skinny jeans.

But I don't have time to analyze how the fight for dominance has improved her fashion sense, because she's seen through my bluff. She knows I'm no match for her in my human form. If I threaten her, and she shifts, then she'll know I can't shift. What little power I have here will evaporate in a second, and I'll be at her mercy. I've spent way too much time there, and it's not an experience I want to repeat.

"Shouldn't you have a protection squad if you're going to cross into witch territory?"

"Thank you for your concern."

I ball my fists and fight my rising frustration at the way she always, always evades my questions. "What are you really doing here? I thought you just came to warn me last time and you weren't coming back."

"Warn you? Oh, yes. Of course." She taps her fingertips against her throat, looking almost...nervous. Did I catch her stealing some witch herbs or something?

I pounce on the slight advantage. "You know how these bargains work, Mother. You tell me what you're doing up here, or I'll tell the witches and you can explain it to them."

Mother doesn't correct me, doesn't tell me that the bargains were always an information swap before. She looks at me a long moment, as if seeing me for the first time. Then she sighs and fiddles with her basket handle. "If you must know, I was hoping to run into you." She peers up at me from under her lashes, looking almost shy, and again I am reminded that she's really not very old. A pang of sympathy goes through me—she took a chance on my father, choosing a mate who wasn't a wolf, and now she'll spend the rest of her life alone. Maybe I shouldn't be so rude to her.

But I know better than to let her manipulate me. I crush the thought and glare at her. "Why?"

"I thought... I know we haven't always gotten along, but we can put all that behind us now, can't we?"

I narrow my eyes at her. "Why would we do that?"

"I am still your mother," she says, but she doesn't say it in her usual harsh way, like I'm required to respect and obey her because she decided to run off with her high school sweetheart and be a teen mom.

"Yeah, and last time I heard, you were trying to kill me."

She laughs, that same high, fake laugh. "Don't be ridiculous, Stella. Why would I do that?"

"Oh, let's see, there are so many reasons to choose from. I kind of stopped counting after the first few times you tried to kill me."

"Don't be dramatic," she scolds, waving her hand as if to dismiss all of those petty concerns. "I have no reason to hurt you. I could have brought along a pack of wolves to destroy you if I wanted. But why would I? You're gone from our valley. You're no longer hunting our prey, and I'm acting Alpha."

"A position you stole," I remind her.

"A position I always deserved," she counters. "I was the Alpha's daughter. It made more sense than choosing a random male."

"A dominant male. I thought you wolves put everything on custom."

"Customs can change," she says. "When they're outdated, they should. There used to be a custom for only men to vote. For humans to own each other as slaves. This custom needs to change. And I'm changing it."

"By telling everyone that your daughter is a witch, and anyone who could love her must be under a spell?"

"Many in our pack wanted you gone," she says. "I'm

not heartless, Stella. You know that. It wasn't all bad, when you lived with me, was it?"

I stare at her in disbelief. Has she lost her mind? Harmon warned me she was cracking under the pressure of leading the wolves and keeping him from taking over.

"Oh yeah, in between you trying to murder me, and being your slave, it was a riot," I say at last.

"That's all in the past," she says. "Now that you're not living with the wolves, and you know about everything, I don't have any reason to want you dead. Killing is a last resort, anyway. But no one would have blamed me, after all you've done."

"You get to look good for sparing my life? That shows the pack how merciful and fair you are? To refrain from killing your own daughter? How noble."

"Would you rather I'd called for your death?"

"I'd rather you have let Harmon lead his pack, invite me to be part of it if I wanted. Since I'm your blood, the blood relative of a former Alpha. You said that meant something. Why couldn't I shift into a wolf at the full moon with the rest of you?"

"If I'd agreed with Harmon, there would be no reason for anyone to side with me," she says, as if it's perfectly logical. "A large part of our pack wanted you exiled, if not killed. Who gives those people a voice if Harmon and I agree?"

"So you took their side, even though you don't agree with it, just so people would follow you, and you could contest Harmon?"

"That's how politics work," she says. "If there are no opposing platforms, there is only one choice. That's tyranny. Don't you think it makes more sense to let the pack vote for whoever it wants, male or female?"

"The pack voted for you?"

"They haven't taken the blood oath to support Harmon, if that's what you're asking," she says with a haughty smirk. "And if he keeps causing trouble, I can exile him. He won't like it, but he'll obey me. He's too young and inexperienced to lead. If my taking over has proved nothing else, it's proven that much."

I take a deep, slow breath, resisting the urge to give her a good slap again. "What are you really doing up here?" I ask. "Come to dig up some herbs and make a potion to keep everyone under your control?"

She gives that high laugh again, and it makes me cringe. It's not just unlike my mother, not just fake, but slightly unhinged, the laughter of a mad woman barely maintaining control. "I'm not the one living among witches," she says when she recovers herself. "But now that you mention it, maybe there are things you could learn from them."

"Oh, so that's why you wanted to forget the past, get all friendly with me? So I'll find out some potion recipes for you? I should have known you'd never actually want to know your own daughter."

"Nothing in life is free," she says lightly. "But believe it or not, I do want to know you, Stella. There's no reason for conflict between us anymore. We could be friends."

She looks at me with the strangest expression, almost childlike in its hope.

"I'll think about it," I mutter. I wouldn't trust her with

one fingernail, but I can't see what she'd want from me. I literally have nothing, am nothing.

"Oh, that's wonderful," she says, reaching into her straw basket. "I was hoping you'd say that. I brought you something."

I wait without moving toward her, halfway expecting her to pull out a rattlesnake and throw it in my face. Instead, she pulls out an ivory hair comb. "This belonged to my mother," she says. "I want you to have it."

"Why me?" I ask without moving to take it. "What about Elidi and Zora? You know, the daughters you actually acknowledge as your own?"

"They have plenty of my things," she says. "Besides, you need it."

At her disdainful glance at my hair, I reach up and touch it. Something that feels suspiciously like a dreadlock meets my fingers.

"Fair enough," I mutter, taking the comb from her. It's creamy white and smooth as glass, with swirls of stark white inside it. It looks like something that belongs in a royal museum, not in my calloused hands. I don't know where I'll keep it out here in the forest, but I feel a bit giddy at the thought of having something of my very own.

I want to ask her about shifting, if she knows how I can unblock the ability. But I don't know if I can trust her with that yet, so I settle for something less dangerous. "Have you seen Dad?" I ask. I don't want to care about him, either, but I can't help wondering.

"Yes," she says, making a face. "He's as selfish and hedonistic as ever."

"If he was always like that, why'd you marry him?" I

realize once I've asked that I've always wanted to know this. How could my father love this woman? But also, how could a woman like her be carried away by anything, let alone young love? I try to imagine her as a wild, impulsive, rebellious teenager refusing her father's orders and falling so madly in love that she couldn't see anything else. But I just can't. She's a frosty ice queen, not fiery and passionate.

"That, my dear, is a very long story," she says. "One we'll have to save for another day. I must get back now. When the cat's away…" She smiles, and for a second, I think she's about to wink at me. A wave of *déjà vous* sweeps over me, the way it does sometimes when she's nice to me, and I get a flash of what it would be like to be her child, one she acknowledged as her own blood. As always, it's unsettling.

12

"My mother came by today," I tell the others that night, as we sit huddled on the log. The sky hangs low and ominous over us, thick with clouds, but somehow it seems brighter than the frigid, starry nights we've had lately. A strange humidity clings to us, making me even colder than usual.

"What?" Xela says, turning to me with wide eyes.

"What did she want?" Uzula asks.

"She was acting kind of odd," I admit. "She said she wanted to be friends."

"She wants more than that," Haven says, nodding wisely. I wonder how old these people really are. "You just wait. You'll see."

"You said you'd hide if she came back," Kale says quietly, frowning into the fire.

I know better than to mistake his concern for affection now. He worries about everyone, but it doesn't mean the same thing to him as it does to me. An invitation to sleep with him is just that—nothing more. I've learned over the past few weeks that I'm the only one who always sleeps alone.

"She didn't hurt me," I say. "She didn't even threaten me. She just acted sketchy. She even gave me a gift."

"You didn't take it, did you?" Kale asks.

"Tell me you didn't," Haven says.

"She took it," Yorn says, shaking his head like I'm just that predictably stupid.

"It's just a comb," I say, slipping it from my pocket.

"Just watch, she'll want something from you now," Haven says. "One hundred percent guaranteed. She'll be back within the week, asking for something in return. You never take a gift from an evil queen. Now you owe her."

"I don't owe her," I say. "It's an heirloom, passed down from her mother. And like she said, I'm no threat to her now."

"Maybe she really does want to be your mother now," Xela says with a sympathetic smile.

"Be careful," Kale says, frowning at me. He puts his hand on my knee, his big sad eyes meeting mine.

"I was careful," I say, annoyed. I move my knee away from his hand, ignoring his wounded look. "It's just a comb. I have nothing she could want. This is literally the only thing I own. And I like it, so I'm keeping it."

"Suit yourself," Haven says with a shrug. "No one's trying to take it away from you."

"Not like you'd tell her if you were," Yorn mutters.

"What?" Haven asks, looking stunned. "I never took anything from you."

"Not from me," Yorn grunts.

"From who?" she asks, her eyes narrowing. "Xela? Uzula? Kale? Have I ever laid a finger on anything you owned?"

A chorus of no's answers her. I am reminded, as I often am, how I don't exactly belong here, either. They all know each other so well, and I don't. I am grateful for their friendship, but aware that I'm still an outsider, as I was at my mother's. The only place I really belong is with my father, in the shifter valley, but I'm not ready to forgive him yet.

After a bit of grumbling, the group falls silent. Everyone goes back to their nests as soon as dinner is over, not lingering to tell stories or gossip as they usually do.

A light snow dusts the ground when I wake up the next day. I pull on my mother's boots, which are a size too small for Haven. Now I know why Mother always wore these work boots—they are comfortable and protective against the sharp rocks hidden under leaves in the forest. But they're not equipped for tromping around in the snow, and as I wander looking for edibles, kindling, and firewood, wetness seeps into them. Soon, my toes are damp and aching with cold. To distract myself, I start humming the tune to a song Dad used to sing when I was growing up. The others were right—I totally hum to myself. I've been more careful not to do that since they made fun of me.

But a second later, it seems to gain a tinkling, musical note. I don't sound half bad. I stop singing and cock my head, listening. I only hear the pure, sweet note echoing. Cautiously, I begin again. This time, I hear it clearly, a voice accompanying my humming. It even makes up for my deficiencies by stretching the notes out in a pleasing way, leading me back to the correct note.

I go on another minute, so pleased by our strange harmony that I let it carry me away. When I come to my senses, my head snaps up and I listen, my heart hammering, as the sweet note echoes through the barren woods. When I look up, I see that same auburn-haired girl who haunts my nightmares, stealing my second nature away after only a taste of what it was like. This time, she's not getting away.

She catches my eye, and for a heartbeat, neither of us move. She looks as startled as I am, as if she didn't notice she was singing along with another person. In one hand, she holds a cloth sack, and she's wearing clothes for once. This is my chance. Before she can escape, I leap after her. At my sudden movement, she turns and runs. But for once, I'm faster and stronger than someone. I catch up to her in a minute, after slipping on the snow-slick leaves a dozen times. I grab the back of her sweater and push her to the ground, keeping my hands tight on her shoulders so I can grasp whatever animal she turns into if she tries to escape that way again.

"Who are you, and what did you do with my tiger?" I ask, pressing her face into the snow and leaves.

"Let me go," she shrieks, twisting under me. I raise myself enough to flip her onto her back, then pin her shoulders again.

"Give me back my shifting," I growl.

"I don't know what you're talking about," she says, spitting snow at me.

"You put some kind of spell on me," I remind her. "I was a tiger, and now I can't shift. What did you do to me?"

"Oh, that," she says, scowling up at me. She has fair, flawless skin, and her hair looks more red than brown against the snow. She's about my age, but definitely not used to working hard like most people around here, if her waifish presence under me is any indication.

"Yes, that," I say, narrowing my eyes. "Whatever you did, undo it."

"I can't," she says simply.

"What? Why not?"

"Because," she says. "I'm the shifter heir, not you."

I pull back a little, cocking my head to peer down at her. "What do you mean, you're the shifter heir?"

"I'm the true heir," she says, her chin rising and a stubborn set tightening her pink mouth.

"Okay, cool, because I have no intention of challenging you for that spot," I say. "I'm not the heir to anything, and I don't want to be. I just want to be a tiger."

"That's what she said you'd say."

"Who is *she?*" I ask. "My mother?"

"No," she says, looking at me like I'm nuts. "Mother Dear. My mother."

"Who's your mother?" I ask, remembering my mother wandering around in the field next to the lighthouse, and how weird she acted. Was she visiting this girl? Feeling guilty about hiding it from me?

"You know who my mother is," she says, beginning to struggle again. "I know you know her, because she talks about you all the time."

"Who? What's her name?"

"Yvonne," she says, her childlike voice growing huffy.

"Mrs. Nguyen?" I ask, sitting up straight, forgetting to hold her down. She wriggles around, then sits up and pushes me off. I fall into the snow, too confused to fight her.

81

"That's not her name," she says, jumping to her feet and brushing angrily at her snowy skirt. "But I guess you wouldn't know that, since you're not from here. You shouldn't have ever come back. *I'm* the shifter princess, and you can't take it away from me."

"I wasn't trying to," I say, clambering to my feet. "You're the one who took my shifting away."

"Good," she says. "If you got it back, you'd probably say you were the heir, and you're not. I am. That's why I can't let you be a shifter, because then you'll try to usurp me."

"I have no interest in ruling anyone," I say. "Now reverse your spell."

"No," she says. "I'm never undoing it. You might change your mind."

I lunge for her, but she shrieks and twists away. She takes off running, but in a few steps, her clothes tumble to the ground, apparently empty. I search through them, looking for a bird or a frog or something, but she's vanished as if she were never there at all.

13

The next day, I'm up in the trees, stuffing long braids of grasses between the branches of our nests so the chilling wind won't blow in, when I hear someone calling. My head snaps up, and my heart stammers in my chest. I must have misheard. But then I hear it again, that lilting voice, calling my name. For a second, I remember all the times I heard that voice calling my sister, while I was locked away in my mother's attic. Before I can sink into the tumult of feelings from that time, I jump up and race across the branches, as reckless as if I could still turn into a tiger and catch myself.

"Stella," Harmon says, a look of relief sweeping over his upturned face when he catches sight of me. He greets me with a wide smile, his white teeth stark against the dark tan of his skin, the corners of his eyes crinkling as he squints into the harsh winter sun. Laughing, I grab a vine and swing down, throwing my arms around him the second my feet touch the ground.

"What are you doing here?" I ask, pulling back.

"Not happy to see me?" he asks, a teasing sparkle in his ice-blue eyes.

"So happy," I say, standing on tiptoes to give him a quick kiss. "But seriously. Won't you get in trouble for coming up here? Or…are you here with good news?"

His face clouds, and I instantly regret ruining our moment of happiness.

"Unfortunately not," he says, stepping out of my embrace but taking my hand. I already ache for more, to press my body against his again, to be closer. I've missed him so much, though I try to put it out of my mind. Even when I manage to think of other things, he's always there, like the sun behind the clouds on a grey day. I need him like a plant needs sun.

"Is it okay for you to be here, then?" I ask. "Won't my mother say that you're betraying the pack, or stage a coup while you're gone?"

"She's pretty much already done that," he says. "She's divided our pack, which is worse than taking it away from me. If they all agreed to follow her, I'd accept it. But the pack is one. It shouldn't be torn apart this way. I hate to see this happening to them."

"Don't packs ever split?" I ask.

"Large ones," he admits. "But we're not that big. Not big enough to hold off the shifter attacks if we don't stand together."

I sigh in frustration. "I wish there was something I could do."

He looks at me a long moment, and I know what's coming before he says it. "There is one thing."

"Harmon…"

"You're my mate," he says, squeezing my hand. "I told you about the prophecy. If we have the mating ceremony, we'll unite the pack with the shifters. They can't deny I'm their Alpha then."

"I'm not sure I'm a shifter anymore," I whisper, not meeting his eyes.

He slides a hand over the top of my head, cupping the back of my neck and pulling me in for a gentle kiss. "You're a shifter," he says with a little smile. "My tigress."

"But I'm not anyone to the shifters," I say. "What about that girl they wanted you to marry? The redhead."

"She's not even a shifter," he says. "And you're my mate. I Chose you."

"I...I can't shift," I tell him. "There's this girl, she took away my ability to shift."

He pulls back and looks at me. "Into anything?"

I nod. "She says she's the shifter heir, that she'll be their leader. And she's afraid I'm going to take her place if I can shift."

"Who?" he asks, looking at me funny.

"I don't know," I say. "I've seen her in the woods more than once. I think she lives in that lighthouse."

"There's no door," he points out. "No one can get in."

"She shifts into a bird," I tell him. "She says she's Mrs. Nguyen's daughter." It's still hard for me to imagine that the frumpy old cat lady who lived next door all my life is someone's mother. Someone my age.

"Then she's a witch, not a shifter."

"She's definitely a shifter," I say. "I've seen her shift."

He looks puzzled. "But the shifter king is your father, and their rulership is passed down familial lines. Is she... your father's daughter?"

"I don't know," I whisper, shaking my head. I don't want to think about my father hooking up with a woman old enough to be my grandmother. But then, that's not her real form, her real body. She told me as much, that she was just borrowing the body.

"There's no way," he says, shaking his head. "They'd have to be married. The shifters won't take his illegitimate daughter if his real daughter is right here."

"They might. Elidi is a werewolf, not a shifter. And if I'm not a shifter, and she's really his daughter…" I break off and shake my head. "And besides, I don't even know them. I didn't grow up here."

"That doesn't matter," he says. "You're the rightful heir. You have royal blood."

"I don't want to lead a bunch of shifters."

"It's your birthright," he says. "Whether you want it or not."

"Well, my father is still their king," I say. "So it doesn't matter."

"It matters," he says. "We can unite the valleys."

I scuff my toe in the leaves, still slushy with snow. "The pack hates me."

"They don't hate you," he says, squeezing my hand. "They're scared of you. They've seen what you can do, and it scares them. But they'll accept you, if it means the end of the shifter attacks. If it means we can all live in peace." He pulls me in, cupping my face between his hands. "Be my mate, Stella. I need you."

I swallow hard. "What if I can never shift again? Now that I know what it's like, I'll go crazy if I can't. And she won't undo the spell. I've asked."

"I don't care," he says. "I loved you before you were a tiger, and I'll love you after. There's nothing you can do to stop me."

I smile a little, but my heart isn't in it. "Okay."

"Right now, it's enough for me to marry the tiger princess," he says, still holding my face. He smiles at me, making me meet his eyes. "Your father can introduce you to them, and they'll get used to you. They'll love you, too, just like I do. And one day, you'll lead them, when you're ready. It doesn't have to be today."

"I'll think about it," I say. "I need to talk to that girl again."

He grins, triumph in his eyes. "We'll be the best Alphas our packs have ever seen," he assures me. "I won't let anyone tear apart our pack. I'm the great uniter, not the divider. And we're going to make this work. I promise."

I nod, my throat suddenly tight. He believes in me so hard, more than he should. He believes in what he says, believes things will work out for us, for the good of everyone. If only I could believe it, too.

14

Too soon, Harmon has to go back to his pack. As I watch him walk away, my insides twist into knots. Could I really go with him, marry him, and expect everything to work out for the best? Nothing in my life works out for the best, so it's a little naïve to start expecting it now. But I can't stand to watch him go. I have to hold onto a tree trunk to keep myself rooted in place, so I won't run after him, tell him to come back or take me with him.

But I have a feeling that if we went ahead with the mating ceremony, the wolves would not welcome me as readily as he thinks. They'd probably throw us both out, now that my mother has half their loyalty. It would be the proof she needs to show that I'm bewitching him.

That night, the snow begins again. It falls quick and steady, huge white flakes that stick on our shoulders and decorate our hair.

In the clearing, Xela stretches out her short arms and spins around and around, head thrown back and tongue out like a child. There is no wind, just the downward rush of white, as if the sky is falling. The others jump around, excited by the prospect of sledding the next day. I can't help but join in.

"Let's do a snow dance," Haven cries, grabbing my hand. I grab Uzula's, and we make a circle around the fire, dancing and kicking snowflakes and singing off-key. Even Yorn tromps around the circle with us, his weathered face cracking into a rare smile as he holds onto Haven's other hand. Excitement buzzes through the air, and we stay at the fire until late into the night. Everyone shares their stories of one winter or another.

I only saw snow in Oklahoma a couple times in my life, and what I've seen here has been from an upstairs window. This is the first winter I'll spend here as a free person, able to enjoy things like sledding and snowball fights and all the other things I wasn't allowed to do when I lived in Mother's attic.

I wonder what the girl in the lighthouse is doing. Is Mrs. Nguyen—Yvonne, I remind myself—there with her? Is she with her mother, or all alone? I've never actually seen Yvonne's real form. I hope the girl is not alone on this cold night, when I am here enjoying the company of friends. I know what it's like to be alone, watching from the outside.

Tonight at last, I feel like I might finally be one of them, or at least on my way. For the first time, I think I am beginning to fit. It wasn't instant, as if I'd come home to my tribe. But now that I've been here over a month, I'm falling into their patterns, their lives. The only thing I'm missing is a place in Haven's collective, a human connection.

If only Harmon could live here with me. If my mother

succeeds in becoming Alpha, he could join me. But I know this wouldn't be enough for him. It wouldn't make him happy. He's a leader, and he needs a pack. That's his nature, his purpose. I should probably do the kind thing and set him free, but I can't bring myself to do it again. Once was bad enough.

When we get up to leave, the fire is nothing but embers in the ring. Xela pulls us around the circle to say goodbye to Doralice, and I stop in front of her instead of shrinking back this time. I'm not exactly scared of her—I talk to her when I'm preparing food or getting the fire ready for Haven to ignite with a snap of her fingers. But touching the juniper tree still makes my skin crawl.

I take a deep breath and stand straight before her. Xela tweaks one of her branches, says goodnight, and skips away. I reach out my hand and run my fingertips over her needles. "Is that girl in the woods your daughter?" I whisper.

"You are my daughter," echoes inside my head, and I jump. I forgot how strange it feels to have her speaking there, from inside me.

I swallow and slide my fingers through her needles, as if I'm holding hands with her. "But is she your daughter, too?"

"Beware the mirror," echoes in my head.

The mirror? I don't know what to make of that. Is she saying the girl is a mirror, a body-snatcher? Is that really Yvonne, not her daughter? Or is she talking about my mirror, my identical twin, who told my mother where to find me? When I ask, Doralice doesn't respond. I turn to Haven, but she just shrugs. As we tread through the snow,

now ankle deep and still falling steadily, I turn to her. "She told me to beware of the mirror," I tell her. "She's not a mirror, right?"

Haven laughs. "Of course not. The spirits in the enchanted forest are people who already died. Doralice's body is buried under that tree."

I remember my mother telling me the same thing. At least she told the truth about something, as insignificant as it was.

We hurry back to the hive, huddled inside our clothes against the chill. The night is lit with an eerie brightness from the snow as we swing up through the familiar trees to our nests. I notice Haven slipping through the branches towards Uzula's nest, and I shiver against a sudden breeze. More than anything, I wish Harmon was here to hold me through the long, cold night. But like every night, I go to bed alone except for the memory of his body beside mine.

15

Sometime in the night, I wake to the sound of the wind shrieking through the trees. I sit up, my heart racing. Something woke me. For a minute, I listen, trying to control my breath, praying it was a nightmare. But I hear the scraping of something against the bark of my tree. What if that crazy girl in the lighthouse decided I'm still a threat, and she needs to get rid of me?

Quietly, I pull down the zipper of my fur-lined hammock and step out. Stripes of snow cut across the branches of my nest, blown in on the howling wind. Slipping my shoes on, I clamber out the opening and look down. A shadowy figure clings to the base of my tree, scrabbling to climb up.

Instantly, my tiger stirs inside, growling to get out. I reach for her, but she sticks there, like something caught in my throat. I want to scream in frustration as the figure scrapes shoes down the tree trunk, searching for purchase. If it was someone from the collective, they would come to my nest from the canopy, traveling by branch and vine, as we all do. For a minute, I watch, my heart hammering. But I cannot dislodge my tiger, bound tight inside me.

A punishing wind streams through the trees, swaying the dead branches, twigs scraping and clicking together like skeletal fingers. Below, a tendril of hair escapes the hood of the climber's coat, and I know it's a girl, not Harmon coming to surprise me.

"Who is it?" I ask, my voice harsh against the howling wind. "I have a weapon."

"Stella," my mother says, sounding relieved. "I didn't want to yell out and wake the others. Come down."

"What do you want?" I ask, more sharply than I expected. I'm still boiling with resentment that she's trying to displace Harmon. Not to mention the fact that she kept me chained up in her attic, refused to let me join the pack, and treated me like a disease.

"I wanted to talk to you," she says. "We're friends now, aren't we?"

"Why are you sneaking around in the middle of the night?"

"What? I can't hear you over the wind. Come down so we can talk."

"What do we have to talk about?" I ask, but I step down onto the next branch. I hate her, but for some reason, I am drawn to her. She's my mother, a part of me. She holds the key to who I am. I'm made up of equal parts her and my father, a mixture of coldness and cruelty, hedonism and irresponsibility.

And if I'm honest, a part of why I take the branch and swing down to the ground isn't just curiosity. I want to punish her. I want to shove it in her face, the way she treated me, the way she always made me feel less than my sisters, less than human. I want her to see how much it hurt me, and to feel guilty for it. And I want it to hurt.

"So, what do you want to talk about?" I ask when I reach the ground. The snow no longer falls in big, soft flakes. It rakes across my cheeks, mean little pellets. It only makes it easier for me to be angry at my mother for dragging me out of bed.

"Let's walk a little," she says. "So we don't disturb your little band of merry misfits." She's wearing a fur-lined navy parka and jeans tucked into tall, lace-up snow boots. I'm wearing a pair of patchwork pants that I slept in and my mother's boots. She doesn't mention it, if she notices.

"You make it sound so fun and frivolous," I say, turning away from her. "In case you forgot, I'm only living here out of desperation, because I have nowhere else to go. Because you told me if I came back, you'd kill me."

She laughs, that weird, nervous laugh. "Surely I didn't say that."

"Not in so many words," I admit. I find myself leading her away from the hive, towards the clearing. The snow is deeper than my ankles now, almost halfway up my shins. It swirls in patterns in front of us, kicked up by the wind, making shapes like ghosts. I shiver and huddle into the black trench coat Haven brought in a bag of clothes last week. I don't ask where she gets things, but I don't think it's by entirely honorable means.

"I've apologized," my mother says behind me. "I never meant to hurt you."

"You just never cared if you did," I point out. "You only care about yourself. You're just like dad."

"Oh, he's not all bad," she says with that high laugh, almost carefree. It's not something I think she's capable of, and it comes across as a lunatic laugh.

"You've seen him?" I ask, unable to stop myself. My time of running away is over. Now I want answers.

"He does live just over the mountain," she says.

I slow as we reach the clearing. "Does he...did he have another daughter?"

"Why do you ask?" she says, sounding more like her old self.

I'm not sure I should tell her, but if I don't tell her, I won't find out what I want to know. It's a risk I'm willing to take. "I saw a girl in the woods," I say. "She's a shifter. She says she's the heir to the shifter throne."

Mother steps past me, approaching the fire pit, where the snow has melted, leaving a bare ring of black stones. She bends and stirs the ashes until an ember glows. "Let's get this going," she says. "I'm sure we could both use some warmth. We can sit and talk."

"Who's the girl?" I insist. "Is she Yvonne's daughter? That's why you hate Yvonne—not because she's dangerous, but because Dad cheated?"

Ignoring me, she goes to the edge of the clearing. The wind has swept the snow from every branch, so the trees are stark and bare. She begins to break limbs and twigs from a pile of fallen trees Kale hauled into the clearing with his freakish faerie strength.

With a sigh, I give in and help her. I can't make her talk. I can only hope she knows the answers to my questions, that she'll share them now that I'm not a threat. I can't see what she'd gain by hiding these things from me. It only strips me of importance, if I don't have the option of being a shifter leader someday, and my powerlessness is something she's never hesitated to reinforce.

When the fire is crackling, she throws on more wood, until it's blazing higher than I've ever seen it. This is not a cooking fire, it's a roaring bonfire. We stand next to it, warming our hands as the wind whips the smoke and sparks across the clearing towards Doralice.

"Tell me about the girl," I say. "You obviously know who she is."

"Why does it matter?" she says, casting a hateful glare in Doralice's direction. "Shift into a tiger and eat her for all I care."

I take a step back, appalled. Yes, I know, that's what I was about to do when she put the spell on me in the first place. But it was different then. My human side was buried deep down inside. I was a tiger, hunting on instinct. And even then, if I had known she was a person, I wouldn't have eaten her.

But my mother hasn't only been an animal for a few months. She's been a vicious wolf all her life, and killing is part of that. I shiver, thinking of Harmon down there, refusing to give his position to her. What if she gets tired of waiting and goes for the kill?

"I can't," I say, shoving my hands into my pockets. "She took away my ability to shift. You could have warned me she was out here. I had no idea. And now I'm stuck like this, because she feels threatened by me."

"She is your father's daughter," she says after a long pause. "But she was raised by witches. That's how she knows such sorcery."

"Why didn't you raise her?" I ask. "Or why didn't Dad, if she was his kid?"

"Oh, you know your father," she says, as if this is some inconsequential matter. When will I stop finding out these horrible things about my family? I have another sister, a half-sister like Zora. A sister my father abandoned, the same way my mother abandoned me. Except she wasn't left with one of her parents. She was left with strangers.

No wonder she's pissed that I'm around. I had a father all those years, and she didn't. And why—because he couldn't be bothered?

"If she's a shifter, too, why didn't he take both of us when he moved to Oklahoma?" I ask.

"Why don't you ask her?" she says, sneering at Doralice. "It had nothing to do with me."

She's my sister. I have another sister. Three years ago, I didn't even know I had one, and now I have three. Granted, they all kind of suck, but still. *Sisters.* My whole life, it was just me and Dad. Now I have this big, complicated family.

"How do I break her curse?" I ask. "Should I ask Mrs. Nguyen?"

My mother's lips twitch in a strange way, like she's trying not to laugh. "If you can't shift, why don't you try projecting into an animal?" she asks at last.

"Harmon says it's dangerous."

"Oh, what does he know?" she asks scornfully. "It probably would be for him. But he's weak compared to you."

"How do you know? I've never done it."

"You've done it," she says with a sly smile.

Mrs. Nguyen told me the same thing. She said I was a natural. "Maybe when I was a baby or something," I mutter.

"You're naturally gifted," Mother says, her golden eyes glittering with some strange emotion. In the firelight, they seem to glow from within. "It would be easy for you. As easy as shifting. Try it."

"I don't know how," I say slowly. "Plus, what would I try it on? Doralice?"

Her eyes sparkle even brighter. "Not a tree, stupid girl," she snaps. "There's an owl in that tree over there. Think of it. Feel it, and push yourself into it."

"But I'd kill it, wouldn't I?"

"Do it," she commands, grabbing me roughly by the shoulders and shaking me. "If you're so good at it you can be a mirror from near infancy, this should be a piece of cake for you. Stop being so stubborn and just project."

"Get off me," I cry, jerking away. "What's your problem?"

She stares at me, breathing hard, her eyes shining. "When you were barely more than a baby, you took over an adult's body and wouldn't give it back. Don't tell me you don't know how."

"No," I say, stumbling back a step. "I didn't do that. I couldn't have. I'd remember."

"But you did," she says, spitting the words at me with such hatred I flinch. "You are the most gifted projector I've ever seen. I've spent my life trying, and I can barely do it even now. But you...oh, you're just so special. So why won't you show me how?"

"Who did I kill?" I ask, my voice cutting through the cold air. The clearing seems to fall silent. The shrieking wind, the crackling, blazing fire, it all freezes around us.

"You were strong enough at three years old to hold out an adult when they wanted their body back," she hisses. "I can't do that. So how did you?"

"Who?" I ask, my voice hard. "It was Doralice, wasn't it?"

Her laughter pierces the momentary stillness, even more hysterical than before. "Not Doralice, you imbecile," she says. "Your grandfather. Your Alpha."

A shock wave rolls through me, through the clearing. And suddenly, it all makes a terrible, chilling sense. I want to deny it, to scream that it's not true, to cover my ears and push the words out so I never heard them. But I know.

This is why she hates me. Why she distrusts me, why she said I was dangerous and kept me locked up in the attic. This is why the pack treated me like a poisonous freak. Because I am. I killed their leader, their god, before I even knew how to speak.

They will never let me walk among them. Not only did I wound their last Alpha and make him too weak to fight back, so that he was killed in a battle with the shifters. Not only did I seduce their current candidate for Alpha. I murdered the one before.

My own grandfather. My own blood.

No wonder everyone was wary of me, no wonder they all wanted me locked away. Without even meaning to, I killed their leader, the most powerful wolf in their pack. Probably without much effort at all. They have reason to hate and fear me.

I don't just look like a mirror because I'm an identical twin. I *am* a mirror. I killed someone in a gruesome way, ripped his soul from his body and stole the body for my own use. For how long—a day? A few hours? Minutes? I was three. I probably thought it was a toy.

No one should have that much power.

But now... Now it all makes sense. My mother has every right to hate me. I am truly my mother's daughter. I am a monster.

Something loosens inside me, and this time, I grab her shoulders. "Why didn't you tell me?" I scream, shaking her. "You let me think they hated me for no reason."

"I'm giving you this power now," she says. "You could thank me for it. The power of knowing you have this amazing, rare gift. Now you know what you're capable of. Use it wisely."

"I don't want this gift," I scream at her. "It's not a gift at all, it's a curse."

She yanks away from me, stumbles, and topples into the plume of fire shooting up from the pyre she built in the fire ring. Sparks explode into the night, mingling with the pelting icy snowflakes. Logs topple from the ring, sizzling in the snow. My mother screams, leaping from the fire. Flames lick along her jacket. Her eyes are mad with pain and fury.

Stunned, I don't move until she grabs me and hurls me towards the fire. I cling to her arms, wrestling to stay on my feet. Twisting in my grip, she forces me towards the fire, even as flames consume her quilted coat. "I bet you'll remember how to project if I throw you into the fire," she growls, digging her nails into my arms and dragging me closer to the flames. "Then you'll have no choice. Do it or die."

She hurls me toward the pit, but I spin away at the last moment. I fall to my knees at the edge of the stone ring, my knee slamming down on one she dislodged from the ring when she fell. With a scream, I roll away just as she leaps at me like a flaming devil. Without thinking, I kick a blazing log from the edge of the fire into her path. She falls hard, her flaming jacket snuffed by the thick snow.

"I didn't mean to kill your father," I say, scrambling away from her. "That was an accident. You are choosing to do this."

"I don't care about that, you stupid whore," she screeches, staggering to her feet. She kicks the log back at me, still ablaze. If only Haven were here, she could throw fire with her bare hands. But there are no witches here to save me, no fae, no wolves. It's just me and my mother.

I step aside as the charred and smoldering log rolls across the clearing. The murderous look in her eyes reflects back my own fury. All this time, she could have told me. All this time, she hated me for a reason.

Well, I have plenty of reason to hate her, too.

As she lunges at me, I grab an unburned branch sticking out of the fire and yank at it. The log attached to it is heavy, but I drag it free amid a shower of sparks and coals. I hardly notice them raining at my feet as I heave it towards my mother. She ducks, then reaches in and grabs the end of another branch, drags it from the flames, and thrusts the burning end at me.

"Is this your idea of friendship?" I taunt, dodging the glowing coals forming along the log. "Gee, Mom, I don't know why we didn't try it before."

She raises the branch over her head and hurls it at me. "You stupid child," she sneers. "You think you're some-thing special because you can project? You killed the wolves' last two Alphas. Do you really think they're going to let you anywhere near Harmon?"

"Too late," I say, darting in to knock her away from the fiery blaze. "He's already Chosen me."

"Don't be naïve," she snaps. "It's not cute. They'll never let you go through with it, not after what you've done."

"Then we'll do the ceremony without the pack."

She laughs, snatching another piece of wood from the fire. "Are you really so stupid as to believe Harmon loves you? The only reason he Chose you is to fulfill that asinine prophecy. The moment he finds out you're not the heir, that you can't unite the pack with the shifters, he'll be sniffing around her back door. Just look at yourself. You're a waste of space. You won't project, you can't shift, you've let yourself go until you're not even pretty anymore."

"You're lying," I growl, dragging a long, thick branch from the fire. But somewhere inside me, something flips. What if it's true?

"I'm sure you were good for a little fun while he was healing," she says, her lips twisting into a cruel mockery of a smile. "But don't deceive yourself. You're not the only girl who's warmed his bed while he waited for his turn on the throne. And trust me, you won't be the last. I know how wolves work, for all their talk of mating for life. There is plenty of mating going on before they choose a life partner."

"Shut up," I scream, hurling the branch at her. She ducks, and it sails over her head and smashes into Doral-ice. Sparks burst skyward, and the needles of the juniper begin to crackle and pop as they catch, but I hardly notice.

What she's saying, it's true. Harmon told me he'd been with other girls before me. Has he been with others since?

"The only thing that made you any different was that he thought you'd be the shifter queen," Mother snarls at me. "But you won't. So his desperate bid for Alpha status is gone. He won't have any use for a patricidal shifter who can't shift. If he wants to be Alpha now, he'll do the smart thing and marry someone the pack approves of. And they'd approve of anyone over you."

"Liar," I scream, but my throat is tightening. Smoke chokes my lungs and burns my eyes, and my hands are scorched from the ends of the hot branches. I didn't touch the fire like my mother did, but it still hurts. Even worse, tears threaten behind my eyes. I can't tell if it's the smoke billowing off the fire and off Doralice, but I don't want to find out if it isn't. I won't let Mother have the satisfaction of making me cry, won't let her see that her words hurt.

I turn and run from the clearing, into the woods. The snow squeaks under my feet, the dry leaves crunching beneath it. Behind, I can see flames licking up from the juniper tree, but I don't go back. I can't. She's already dead, anyway.

I stumble along blindly for a time, wanting to put as much distance between myself and my mother as possible. Still, I turn every few minutes and look back, expecting her to follow. But she doesn't. She made her point already.

An orange glow hovers at the top of the mountain, a glow cast by Doralice burning. But I don't stop. So many questions tumble through my mind with the betrayal and hurt and fear. What if she's right? What if Harmon only chose me because he thought I could secure his position?

It's not such a crazy thought. He barely knew me, and he's known everyone here all his life, including my twin. Why not marry her, if she's equally tied to the shifter crown? He chose me, though, because I'm a shifter, because they would claim me instead of my werewolf sister.

After a time, I come out on a dirt road. The entire sky is starting to brighten. Smoke still clings to my skin, my hair, the air, but as morning dawns, my mind begins to settle. I turn and hurry along the road, towards a place that has answers.

16

When I arrive at my father's doorstep, I find the house dark and quiet. Not surprising, since it's barely light out. I feel strange knocking on his door, but I'd feel even stranger if I didn't. So I stand on the porch, waiting for him to come to the door. A flash of *déjà vous* rolls over me, so intense I sway on my feet. Knocking on his bedroom door, tiptoeing in, finding him dead.

Except he wasn't dead, I remind myself, gripping the door knob. He'd projected here, into an animal, and was captured by witches. By Yvonne.

After a minute, I knock harder, refusing to give in and go inside, like I did before. And soon, I hear the creak and thud of footsteps inside. Dad opens the door, pulling a robe tight around himself. He looks older, worn and unkempt. I can't remember if he's changed since last spring, or if I'm still comparing him to the nerdy professor I grew up with, the regular guy, the jokester.

He squints at me, then past me, then lifts his head and sniffs the air. "Fire somewhere," he observes, his eyes narrowed at the trees behind me.

I swallow and drop my eyes, not wanting to admit I burned down his first ex-wife in a fight with the second. "I have some questions," I say, squaring my shoulders. I'm not a little girl anymore, one he can lie to and protect. I've seen enough at seventeen to be an adult.

"You and me both," he grumbles, turning away and shuffling into the kitchen.

At least he doesn't treat me like a kid, yelling at me for running off. But the thought makes me a little sad as I follow him into his cramped kitchen. Dirty dishes clutter the sink, something I would have taken care of if I still lived here. But I refuse to feel guilty. He's a grown man, and if I can take care of myself, he certainly can.

After he puts on a pot of coffee to brew, he comes to the table and sits at the one clear spot, where he probably eats every day. I sit opposite him, pushing aside a pile of catalogs and junk mail.

"You been with your mother?" he asks after a long, awkward moment.

"You could say that," I say, looking down at my hands, smeared black with soot.

"I guess I never was a very good father."

"Dad, you were fine," I say with a sigh. I don't want to get back into this, the way we'd go around and around last spring, with me reassuring him he was great even though, really, he wasn't. But it's the perfect segue into one of the conversations we need to have, so I start there. "I met Doralice," I say, taking a long, steadying breath.

He nods, his gray eyes calculating. "Is that right?"

"Yes," I say. "How come you never told me about her?"

"What did she tell you?" he counters. "Been talking bad about me, I suppose."

"She didn't say anything about you," I tell him.

"Mother told me who she was, or I wouldn't have known. What happened?"

"She died, that's what happened," he says with a scowl. He stands and goes to the counter to pour himself a cup of coffee.

"I'm sorry." For some reason, I had thought she died after the divorce, that he wouldn't care. I didn't mean to prod a painful memory. As selfish as he's been, I can't fault him for keeping this one to himself. When I imagine the pain I'd feel if something happened to Harmon, I know wouldn't want to talk about it, either.

"Is that it?" he asks, opening the refrigerator. He takes out a jar of milk and pours some into two cups of coffee steaming on the counter. Again, my heart tightens at the sight of him treating me like an adult. I used to love coffee, but I had to sneak it when I was at my friend's house, because Dad said I was too young for it.

"No," I say, flattening my hands on my thighs to steady them. This is harder than I expected. I expected him to be mad, or happy, or at least have missed me. But he seems distant, like I'm a stranger. I guess, in a way, we are strangers now.

"There's a girl in the woods," I say. "She says she's the shifter heir. I guess that means she's your daughter, since you're the shifter king." It's hard to say that while looking at this man, with his messy, decrepit house, his overgrown beard and straggly hair, his paunchy middle straining against his worn bathrobe. I picture my mother in her stylish boots, her skinny jeans and parka, her hair in a long braid with a few loose strands framing her heart-shaped face. In comparison, my father looks like a pathetic old man.

Dad brings the cups to the table and sits, his chair creaking under his weight. "Don't have sugar," he says, pushing a coffee cup across the table. "Hope you don't mind it with just milk."

I don't like it plain, but I don't say anything. When he doesn't answer my question, I go on. "She also says Yvonne is her mother. Did you…is she really your kid with Mrs. Nguyen? She's so…old."

He sips his coffee, not meeting my eye. It's clear he doesn't want to talk about any of this. That's why he never told me. Not to protect me, but to protect himself. The old resentment grows, and I ball my hands into fists in my lap.

"It's complicated," he says at last. "But the shifters would accept either of you as their leader." He smiles, his eyes going far away. "Either of you would do a hell of a lot better job than I have."

"You left them for over ten years," I point out.

He flinches, but says, "Not for nothing. I left to raise you."

"Why didn't you take her with us? She's your daughter, Dad. My…sister."

"Her mother wouldn't let me," he said. "She kept me from her. It wasn't my choice."

I can't help but soften towards him. I'm not really interested in ruling anyone, but I had to know. "Okay," I say. "Let's talk about something else. Projecting."

He eyes me suspiciously. "You been doing that?"

"Not yet," I say. "But I've been told I'm…gifted." I choke over the word.

"Your mother tell you about the time you did it before?"

I hold my coffee cup between both hands, my eyes fixed on it. "Yes."

"Well, then. You know why we all wanted to put a stop to whatever magic you possessed."

"Because I killed my grandfather."

"Uh huh. When your mother and I married, the only way she'd agree to it was if I moved over there, into the wolf community. Would have made more sense the other way around, for her to come here. But she was so attached, a real daddy's girl. You know how wolves are about their Alphas. That loyalty doesn't exist with shifters and their king."

A note of bitterness creeps into his words, but after taking a sip of coffee, he goes on. "I loved Talia, and you and your sister, so I went along with her request. Well, you can guess how much the shifters liked that. I'd abandoned them before I moved to Oklahoma."

"I'm sorry," I say, not knowing what else to say.

He sighs. "It's all right. But they didn't like that I left them. I'd projected before, but Yvonne was the one who really got me interested in it. She was always a bit obsessed with it. And we did have a little relationship of sorts, before your mother and I married. Yvonne didn't always look like Mrs. Nguyen. She was a little obsessed with beauty and youth, too. She'd do…spells and such."

He smiles fondly at the memory, but it still makes me squeamish to think of all those nights they'd sit up late talking in the kitchen, when she was an eighty-year-old woman. Now I *really* know why they were so chummy.

"Well, she hoped it would be passed down genetically, my ease with it. She wanted me to try it with all my kids. You did it without any effort at all, turned into a butterfly when you were two years old and flew out the window. Scared your mother witless."

He laughs while I try to imagine Talia freaking out for my safety. "I guess I was okay?"

"You were fine," he says. "But she didn't like projecting, said it was witchcraft. Wolves are so superstitious, have that whole legend of the mirror, this body snatching spirit that goes through the land taking over people's bodies. But it's not that easy. Most people could never force out a soul from a body—it would have to be a very weak or broken one, like Mrs. Nguyen. That's how Yvonne was able to enter her body—because she was already dying."

"But I did it," I say quietly.

"Yeah, you did," he says, sounding almost proud. "Your mother told me never to coach you in projection again, but we did it anyway. Our little secret." He winks at me, as if this is some fun conspiracy, like we used to have when I was growing up. He always made me feel like we were a team, just us against the world. We'd get away with something, and he'd wink at me like it was an inside joke that only we got.

The coffee suddenly turns sour in my stomach. "You told me to do it?"

"I taught you to do it," he says. "The shifters may not have liked me moving to the next valley, but I brought about peace between the shifters and wolves. A marriage alliance. The wolves let us hunt in their valley. We were peaceful with them, and in exchange, I had to live there and only shift into a wolf with them. But your grandfather wasn't a good man, Stella. He was stingy as hell. He may have fooled your mother, daddy's little girl, but he didn't fool me. So when you got a little older, I told you to project yourself into him when I knew he was sleeping. I thought I'd make him walk outside and act like a three-year-old, maybe take him down a peg when everyone saw him acting a fool. I figured he'd wake up and pop you right out. That's how it usually works. The soul has a hold on its own body. It knows where it belongs."

My hands are shaking with rage. "But I killed him instead?"

"I never thought you'd be strong enough to hold onto a human body when the soul came back," he says, shooting me a guilty, chagrined smile. Playing the innocent jokester again. "I didn't mean to kill him. But as soon as Zechariah took over, he kicked us out. Said we'd broken the truce, since they let shifters in and we ended up killing their leader. They were pretty pissed at us both. And the shifters were pissed we'd broken the truce and they couldn't hunt in the wolves' valley, so they were out to get us, too. It was safer to go somewhere else, hide out a while. I always meant to come back when things settled down."

"But you never meant to tell me all this?" I rise from the table, gripping the edge to steady myself. A siren wails in the distance.

"Now what kind of father tells his daughter she's a murderer?" Dad says, holding up his hands in supplication. "You would have thought you were a monster. We had a good run in Oklahoma City. We had some fun, didn't we?"

"I'm not the murderer," I say, the words hard as the balls of ice clicking against the glass panes. "You used me to do your sick business. You're the murderer. I'm the weapon."

Lights flash against the window. For a second, my heart stops. I might know the truth, but to the world, I'm the one who killed my mother's father. Momentarily confused, I think she's called the police and told them. That's why she didn't follow me. But a long red truck sails by, red lights circling. Behind it, another one.

When I turn back to Dad, he's standing, too. And for the first time in my life, I'm afraid of him, too. He's older than my mother, out of shape. But he's still a foot taller than me, a big man all around.

But his eyes aren't angry anymore. He looks scared as he cranes to see out the kitchen window.

"Forest fire," he says.

"But…it's snowing."

"Dry leaves, strong wind," he says. "It's got plenty of fuel."

I shake my head, stepping back. First I killed my grandfather, then I might as well have killed Harmon's father, and now I've burned down their forest? I'm like a curse on the Lunessa pack.

And then a dart of ice pierces my heart.

Harmon.

Without a word, I race for the door, out into the snow. It stings my face, shocking after the warmth of my father's house. I race for the road, where the next fire truck is making its way around the treacherous curves, on the slippery snow.

Why didn't I think of this before? Because it's winter, and fires happen in the summer? Or because I was too angry?

I curse the girl in the woods, the one who made me slow and clumsy. If I could shift, I could race the truck to the valley. But now, I'm just a human. Smoke churns in the air, and ashes shift down with the snow.

Why didn't I put out the fire in Doralice?

"Thank you."

I spin around, opening my mouth to answer, when I realize the voice was inside me. I whip around the other way, looking for a tree, but there is nothing.

"You set me free," Doralice says in her dreamy, spooky voice. "Thank you."

I turn again, only to see my father staring up into the mixture of snow pellets and ash drifting down. "Come on," I say, gesturing frantically. "We have to help them."

Without waiting for an answer, I turn and run.

17

When we reach the top of the mountain, the smoke is so thick my eyes stream with tears. Dad is gasping for breath beside me, his shirt pulled up over his nose and mouth. Below, we can see the firetrucks trying to contain the fire. But even from here, with the sky as dark as twilight from smoke, we can see it's too late for the wolves. Half of their beautiful little valley, peaceful and full of so many trees the green of them hurts your eyes in summer, is in flames.

Panic washes over me when I think of them down there, in their little log cabins. Elidi, my twin. Zora and Mother, their friends, their pack. And Harmon.

"Come on," I say, leaping forward, down the slope. My feet slide in the snow, now covered in a grey crust of ash, but I don't stop. I slide and tumble and race down the mountain. Within the wolf valley there are other hills and ridges and folds of land. But I head straight for the cabins. The firetrucks are close now, containing the fire. Later, they'll probably say it was only a small one, only one mountainside burned. One mountainside, and a handful of cabins that belongs to that crazy cult who never left their valley.

I would have said the same thing when I arrived. But now I know better. It's not just a crazy cult in their secluded valley. It's a pack of wolf people, violent and brave and scared and naïve. Their homes that they built by hand, everyone in the community pitching in. Their mountainside, that they use for hunting when they turn into wolves, so they won't have to hunt elsewhere and kill people's livestock or trespass onto their land. The valley they plant crops in, pick apples in, provide for themselves in. They are completely self-sufficient—because of this valley.

I come out of the woods near the road, which means I have to duck back so the firemen won't see me. I sprint towards the cabins, along the clearing where the wolves gather every month as they transition into animal form. Through a short stretch of woods and out onto a dirt trail. The heat of the fire shimmers on the mountainside, scorching my skin, roaring like a thousand tigers. I duck back into the woods to avoid being seen by a firetruck that's inside the little circle of cabins. Pulling my shirt over my nose, I race down the slope to my mother's cabin.

It's been over six months since I was here, but it feels like a day. Nothing has changed—not the lamp I fixed that now sits at the end of the couch, or the smell of wood and dust and home that clings inside the house.

"Mother," I yell, my voice coming out hoarse. "Elidi!"

No answer. My father clomps up the steps, grasping his chest and wheezing. "They will have gone," he says between gasps for breath. "They've got a keen sense of smell."

"They wouldn't just leave," I say, dashing up the stairs. "They'd stay and defend their homes." It strikes me then that I know these people. I may not like them, but I know them better than anyone in the world—better than the rebels on the hill, better than my own father. Despite everything, they were my family, my community.

I burst into Zora's room and find it just as it always was, the bed neatly made up with the flowered quilt. Dad is right about this one. I can tell by the feel of the house that no one is here. The empty spot above her dresser catches my eye, a spot where she hung the mirror I found in my attic room. A twinge of guilt darts through me when I remember how much she loved that mirror, how she fought to keep it, how selfish I was about it. As horrible as she could be at times, she was just another product of Mother's hatred. I should have been nicer to her, should have seen she loved that mirror enough to haul the heavy thing away from a fire, maybe the only possession she could carry.

Dad yells for me, and I run back downstairs. "You're right," I say. "They're not here."

We leave the house, hurrying through the woods. I look up, and that's when I see it—Harmon's big, beautiful lodge, the one at the very end of the community, is burning. It's the one nearest the mountainside, and now, it's being dowsed with fire hoses, water pouring in through a smoldering hole in the roof. My throat catches, and I push closer, despite the heat. Wet leaves steam under my feet, the snow completely melted by the heat. Outside Harmon's house, I see dozens of people throwing buckets of water.

"It's them," I gasp, my legs almost going out from under me. I can just imagine the firemen telling them to leave, and everyone standing in line, stoically refusing to abandon their leader. They are loyal. No matter what they say, they are here, serving their Alpha.

My Alpha.

Tears well in my eyes as I stumble forward.

"Wait," Dad says, grabbing my arm. "You can't go out there. They'll kill you, Stella."

"I have to," I tell him, pulling my arm away. Above us, a tree crackles with heat. There are no leaves to help spread the fire, which is maybe why it has moved so slowly. But the branches eventually catch, and the one above us begins to smolder before it burns.

"Dad, come on," I urge. "They need our help."

"We've both seen their basement prison," he reminds me. "I don't want to end up there again."

"They won't hurt us for coming to help," I say, pulling him away from the tree as the branches flicker with flames. "If anything, they'll thank us. Think about it. This is your chance to make amends, to show them you've changed. To make another truce."

"A truce?" he says, looking at me like I'm crazy. "Look at this place!" He gestures to the tree behind us, flames now shooting ten feet from the massive branches. My heart twists when I think how old that thing is, probably hundreds of years. For all I know, another ghost like Doralice is trapped inside it, either longing to get out or terrified to finally meet its end.

"I'm going to help," I say, turning to the house.

Dad grabs my arm again. "Don't you see it?" he asks, his eyes almost gleeful. "This time, they'll be begging *us* for a truce. They'll be begging to hunt our land. You're right—we'll make a truce. But this time, we'll make the terms. I'll make them grovel the way they made me. I'll show them what it's like to see their people going hungry, their children crying from cold in the winter, while I turn my back on their pleas for help."

"Dad," I say, horrified.

"That's what they did to us," he says, his eyes dark and hard as coal. "You don't know how bad it was before I married your mother. Why do you think I pushed so hard for it, gave up my valley and moved here for her? For my people. For our people, Stella. You're not a wolf. You don't owe them. You're a shifter."

"I'm also a human being," I say, prying his fingers from my arm. "And they need my help."

I turn and start towards the lodge. When I look back, Dad is walking away. But he must feel my eyes, because he stops under the flaming tree and turns back to watch the fire consuming the lodge, his face a weird mask of delight and malice. A loud crack splits the air, and as if in slow motion, the massive branch above him detaches from the tree and falls. He pitches forward at the last second, but it's too late. He disappears under the inferno of flames.

18

With a scream, I charge back towards Dad. But the heat stops me short of reaching the branch. "Dad," I scream, but I know he's gone. Something inside me feels it, like a slice of my heart is cleaved from the whole.

I scream again, but heat blisters my skin when I try to reach out. Tears streaming down my face, I turn and race into the clearing at the front of Harmon's lodge. I tell one of the firefighters, who must think I'm crazy as I hysterically explain, amid tears and wild gesturing, where my father is. When he goes to investigate, I join the wolves.

"Where's Harmon?" I ask, grabbing the first person I see, my sisters' friend Xiu. Her face is bright red and shiny with sweat, her black hair sticking to her cheeks.

"He went up the mountain," she says. "When it started. He took off that way."

She nods towards the flaming mountain as someone supplies her with a bucket, which she sloshes onto his porch.

I stumble back, my heart in my throat. I can't lose him and my father on the same day. It's too much to bear. Especially since I know why Harmon took off up the mountain —for me. Choking on sobs, I turn and plow into the woods again. I skirt around the fire, staying far enough away that I won't meet the same fate at my father, but close enough to the edge to know that I'm going in the right direction. As I scramble up the mountain, slipping on wet leaves, choking on smoke, I pray for my father, and for Harmon, and all the rest of the wolves. And I swear that the next time I see that bitch who took away my shifting and made me into the slowest creature on earth, I will rip out her heart.

I keep cursing myself as I trudge uphill. Why didn't I stop and put out the fire when it started? My mother didn't, either. She was probably happy to watch Doralice burn. But where is she now? Was she down at the fire, helping save the lodge? Or did I lose her, too?

To my surprise, the thought makes my stomach knot and my tears start again. Yes, she was horrible. But she was still my mother. There was so much I still wanted to know. Who knows, over the next twenty or forty years, how much they could have told me. Things I'll never know, lost forever.

And it's not just what he knew. It's who he was. Yes, he was selfish and gluttonous, irresponsible and defensive. But he was my father. He gave up being a king for me. He took me away from this violent life and gave me a normal life, with curfews, movies with friends, and cotton candy at the fair. He took me to school to meet my teachers at open-house, took me to the doctor when I got sick, took me on father-daughter dates to get root beer floats at old-fashioned soda fountains. He wore socks with sandals, cheesy t-shirts that embarrassed me, and big goofy grins when he told lame jokes. Maybe he didn't deserve to sit on the pedestal I put him on most of my life, but he was still my dad. My very flawed, very human, father.

I arrive at the top of the mountain, my eyes stinging and my lungs aching with smoke. I have to stop, bending over with my hands on my knees, to cough and choke out the rest of my tears. When I straighten, I notice that for the first time since I left my dad's, the air is clear. At first, I think I'm imagining things. But then I realize what it is. The wind is blowing towards the fire, blowing it down the mountain. Clean, clear air is blowing in from the other direction, bringing a few cold, hard snowflakes that sting my scorched face.

That's when I think of my friends up here. Another wash of guilt sweeps over me. In all the panic and concern with the wolves, I didn't even think of my real friends, the ones up here, who took me in without question and never made me feel like a freak. Forcing my aching, leaden legs to move, I jog along the top of the mountain. It's strange how exactly the fire has moved in the other direction. Everything up here is untouched.

When I reach the clearing, I see the charred, blackened remains of a juniper tree, and a deeper sadness sinks in. Again, I think of all the stories that will never be told, that died with Doralice. I know she's dead, like Dad. I felt her spirit leave, too. Not inside me, but that voice thanking me, planting a small seed of gratitude inside me. At least I know she doesn't hate me for what I did to her. It might be nothing—the gratitude of a ghost—amid the destruction of what I caused. But I hold onto it like it's the seed of a new life.

"She lives," a voice crows. I whip around to see Xela charging towards me. Before I can prepare myself, she launches her sturdy little body at me. Together, we topple into the snow. "You look like shit, though."

I wipe at my face, but the back of my hand is black with soot, so I doubt it does much good. Sitting up, I see Haven holding up both hands to the wall of flame, her eyes shining, her black skirt billowing out behind her and her hair whipping around her face. Her feet are planted wide, her fox sitting motionless between them, staring into the fire as if hypnotized. For the first time, I'm witnessing Haven's true power, and it's a little bit frightening. Beside her stand two women I've never seen, and the girl from the lighthouse, all of them chanting and waving their hands in different motions at the flames.

I jump up and run towards them, desperation clawing up my spine. "Stop!" I scream. "You're burning the wolves' valley."

When I get closer, Haven turns, soot smeared across her face like war paint. "Oh, good, you're back. I have something that belongs to you," she says, dropping one hand from her task and reaching behind her, batting at the fabric of her skirt. At first, I think she's putting out a spark, but then she gets her billowing skirt under control and I see the form lying behind her. It blends in with her black skirt and the snow—a black and white wolf.

I cry out and fall to my knees beside Harmon's bound body. "What did you do to him?"

"I didn't do anything but save him from the fire," she assures me. "If he hadn't been hellbent on diving straight into a wall of flame to go searching for you, I wouldn't have had to tie him up like a...well."

"Harmon," I say, grabbing his head. His eyes are wild

and desperate. I tug at the knots, quickly undoing them. The moment he's loosed from the bonds of rope, he begins to transition back to human form. Though I hate the snapping and popping of bones and cartilage rearranging itself, I don't let go. I wrap my arms around his neck and press my face into his fur, not releasing my hold until he's fully human.

"Keep your dog on his leash," one of the other witches says. "We can't have him doing anything to break the spell we're weaving."

Harmon's voice is choked and ragged when he speaks. "Stella," he says into my hair, pulling me into his lap, his hands moving over my body as if to make sure I'm really here, that I'm real. "I thought you were—I thought..."

"Me, too," I say, taking a shuddering breath.

"You're okay?" he asks, loosening my arms and holding me away, taking in my filthy face, my tangled hair, my torn clothing.

I nod, not trusting my voice.

"Where were you?" he asks. "What happened?"

"Dad..." I swallow. "He's gone."

Harmon pulls me into his arms, cradling my head against his chest. "Oh, Stella. I'm so sorry."

Before he can feel too sorry for me, before I can let myself cry and accept sympathy I don't deserve, I blurt out the truth. "It's my fault," I say. "I was fighting with my mother, and I caught a tree on fire. I didn't know it would burn."

Harmon swallows, studying me for a long moment. "We all make mistakes," he says quietly. "Sometimes we do things we don't mean to do, or we don't know what we're doing, or we're forced to do things that might hurt someone we love. I'm sure I'll do things that hurt you sometimes, too. Forgiveness is part of love."

I nod, unable to look at him. What has he done that requires my forgiveness? Mother's poisonous words trickle back to me. But no matter what he's done, it can't be anything compared to what I've done—killed their Alpha, burned down their valley...

I am worse than a curse on them.

"Wait..." I say, drawing away. "What do you mean, we do things we don't mean to do?"

Harmon drops his gaze. "Nothing."

"You knew," I whisper. "You know, don't you? What I did, when I was a kid? Why I was sent away. Everyone knows, that's what she said. She's right, isn't she? You know I'm a mirror."

He swallows, but drags his eyes up to meet mine. "I know."

Betrayal burns through my veins, turning them as cold as his eyes. "Why didn't you tell me?"

"I—I'm sorry."

"That's all you can say? You're sorry? You could have told me, all that time." I start to get up, but he pulls me back.

"For a long time, I had no idea that you didn't know. It was something you did, and I assumed your dad had told you, if not your mom. When you came back, no one here knew that you had never shifted, either. You have to realize, Stella, no one knew anything had been kept from you."

"And when you found out?"

"When your mother told us you weren't aware you were a shifter, or that any of this existed…I guess everyone was afraid of you. Afraid you might get mad and…do what you did to Efrain, your grandfather. If you'd done it by accident before, they thought you could again. They were terrified of you."

"So they treated me like a freak. Lovely."

"Like a loaded gun," he said. "You could kill anyone here, Stella."

"So could you," I explode.

"That's different. We're all the same. You can do something that's sorcery to our people."

"It would have been nice if I'd known that from the start."

"I'm sorry," he says again. "I didn't know how to tell you. How do you tell a person something like that?"

"Um, it goes something like this. 'Hey, by the way, everyone hates you because you killed our last Alpha.' How hard is that?"

"You're right," he says. "I didn't tell you because it was too hard."

His admission melts some of my anger. "I just wish I didn't have to find out from my mother."

"She's probably exactly the person who should have told you," he says quietly. "A long time ago. But it doesn't change anything now. You were barely more than a baby. It has nothing to do with what's happening now."

It's hard to believe that when I can barely hear him over the roar of the fire, a fire I started because I was so furious about finding out. When the pack can't look at me without knowing I'm a killer.

But so what? They fight and kill all the time. It's not so shocking that I killed someone. It's who I killed and how I did it. I vow then that I'll never do this evil thing. Being a tiger is enough. I don't want to be anything or anyone else.

I cut my eyes to the girl who cursed me. "What is she doing here? And what are they doing?" I hiss, nodding my head in Haven's direction. "Are they burning your valley?"

He shakes his head, his eyes sad and resigned.

"We're keeping the fire from the First Valley," Haven says. "By keeping it at bay. We're not making it burn anything. We're just stopping it from spreading this way."

"And what is *she* doing here?" I ask again.

"I'm helping," the girl says in her breathy, childlike voice.

I turn back to Harmon. "That's the girl. The shifter heir."

"Do you want to fight for the position?"

I try to squeeze words past the lump in my throat as I realize that she's not the heir anymore. My father is dead. The shifter king is dead. And she doesn't even know it. I nod mutely, cutting my eyes to the others.

"We should go somewhere and talk," Harmon says quietly.

I lower my voice, too. "What about you? Will the pack see it as a betrayal that you ran off to find me and left them?"

"Maybe," he says with a frown. "Or they might see it as romantic. It depends on if your mother showed up. She was gone when we got wind of the fire."

"You can bet she'll be down there stirring up dissent," I say bitterly.

"I should probably get back, now that I know you're safe," he admits. "Thank you for telling me about this. For being honest. Not everyone would take responsibility like that."

I nod, my body stiffening in his arms. I know there's more.

"We probably shouldn't tell the wolves," he says quietly. "Not yet."

"A lot of the valley burned," I tell him, forcing myself not to sugarcoat it. I know he doesn't want to hear half-truths. "Some of the cabins, too."

He nods, looking pained. "I was afraid of that."

"We can offer a place," says the older witch, the one who told me to keep Harmon leashed. It makes me wonder if she heard everything, my confession included.

"I'll have to see the damage," Harmon says. "Maybe it isn't as bad as it sounds."

"It is," I whisper.

"For now, you are welcome in our valley," the witch says. "If not into our homes, you can make your homes up here until you've recovered. We have plenty, and few hunters. You are welcome to hunt here during the Moon."

"Thank you," Harmon says, his voice strong but humble. "I will let my wolves know they have the option, should their homes be destroyed. I can only hope we don't have need to take advantage of such a generous offer."

I can't help but be impressed by how dignified he manages to sound while sitting naked in the dirt, with me still on his lap.

"Oh, goody," Xela says, clapping her hands. "Lots of newcomers!"

"I should go," Harmon says again, his eyes dropping to mine. "I don't want to, but I should. If you're okay…"

I wrap my arms around his neck and squeeze him hard. I want to help him through this time, want him to help me. But we can't. Hopelessness of the situation cloaks me like a blanket. Will we ever be able to be together?

"I'm okay," I whisper. "Thank you." I don't say more, but I hope he knows that I'm thanking him for more than his concern. That I'm thanking him for his forgiveness, for coming for me when the fire started.

As he shifts back and I let him go, I can't help but feel a twinge of guilt. Because though I've done a horrible thing, a tiny part of me thrills at the idea of him being close again. If the wolves make this mountaintop their temporary home, we'll be together again, even if we have to keep it a secret.

19

Even when the fire is out, it is still with us. For days, the smoke lingers, coating the snow with grey. The smell of it clings to our clothes, our hair, our skin, until I can't remember the smell of anything but burning trees. After a few days, when the last wisps of smoke drift over the far mountain, the other remnants linger. One mountainside is barren except for the twisted, charred remains of trees, now blackened skeletons.

And there are ghosts. The angry spirits that once resided in the trees on that mountainside are free to torment their victims. Astrid, the girl from the tower, sets about putting them into unoccupied trees, but there are more than she can handle in a day. A few times, the ghosts play with us, trailing cold fingers down our backs or blowing into our ears. But mostly, they are silent to all but the ones they haunt. After one of the wolves almost goes mad and tries to off himself, Astrid establishes an order of importance for dealing with the ghosts. I want to confront her again, but right now, her other duties seem more pressing.

The biggest change, though, is that the entire wolf pack makes camp on top of the mountain. Some set up further along the plateau of the mountaintop, where they can remain on their territory, but most camp on the witches' territory, not far from our little encampment. When I ask Harmon why half the wolves didn't stay back, since many of the houses suffered no damage at all, he says that Talia got suspicious when he offered to take the displaced wolves to live on the mountain.

"I don't know what she thinks I'll get up to," he says with a smile.

"I can't imagine," I say, rolling my eyes. "Surely a clandestine mating ceremony never crossed your mind."

"Surely not."

The witches come around more often, too, usually helping the wolves. Despite my hope that I might see Harmon more often, he's almost always down in the valley with all the wolves, beginning to rebuild or repair the houses. After a couple days, I join them. I expect someone to protest, to tell me I should be locked in an attic or strung up by a noose as an example, but for the most part, everyone ignores me.

On my third day in the valley, I end up pulling charred boards from the wall of one of the cabins. When I look over, I see that my sisters are working their way towards me from the other corner of the house. We don't say anything as we draw closer, only continue pulling nails and dropping them into a discard bucket. At last, we're nearly elbow to elbow.

"At least I can tell you apart now," Zora says, looking from Elidi to me. "Seriously, Stella, are their birds nesting in your hair?"

"I think they've migrated for the winter," I say. "But ask me again this spring and I might have a different answer."

"I thought Mother gave you her ivory comb," Elidi says, darting a quick glance at me.

"She did," I say. "I just don't have much reason to use it."

"Um, maybe so you won't look like a crazy person?" Zora suggests.

I shrug. "Not my number one concern."

"It should be," Zora says. "If you want to be an Alpha's mate."

I study her from the corner of my eye, wondering if that's common knowledge. The way she threw it out there, so off-hand, makes me think it is.

"Harmon doesn't care what I look like," I say after a bit. I remember what he looked like, when he was stuck between animal and human, a deformed beast. If I could love him like that, a few tangles in my hair won't bother him. They better not.

"Yeah, but the rest of the pack might," Elidi says. "If you're going to be an Alpha's mate, you have to look the part."

"What is that supposed to mean?" I ask, bristling.

"You're the pretty one," Zora says. "Figure it out."

Elidi glances at her and then fixes her gaze on me. "No one's saying you're not pretty. But he's the wolf representing the pack when outsiders come to talk to us. He'll look the part. And you'll be at his side. No one is saying you have to wear a ballgown and makeup. But you could at least comb your hair and not completely humiliate him."

Stung, I turn back to my work. But after refusing to acknowledge them for the next fifteen minutes, curiosity wins out and I give in first. "So...how have things been, anyway?" I ask. "Harmon and Mother have both come up to visit, but I'm not down here where the trouble is. Is it bad?"

"It's pretty tense," Elidi admits. Some part of her still seems hesitant to talk to me. I can't tell if it's lingering guilt from all the times we had to sneak in a word or two to each other, when Mother kept me prisoner, or if she's still under orders not to speak to me.

"I'd ask who you're supporting, but I'm guessing you're not going to say it out loud," I say. I remember how much they both admired Harmon, and yet...Mother is hard to defy, and they are her daughters. No matter what I think of her, she is their mother. She raised them, and they know a side of her I've never seen, a nurturing side. They must be at least a little torn in their loyalties.

"She'd make a good Alpha, you know," Zora says. "She's very dominant, in case you couldn't tell."

I snort out a laugh as I yank a nail free. "Oh, I can tell."

"And it isn't really fair that only guys get to be Alpha," Elidi says, her voice taking on a defensive edge.

"But do you really think she has the pack's best interests in mind?" I ask. "Or is she just taking advantage of the disharmony in the pack to stake her own claim to someone else's position? Zechariah was your last Alpha, and he gave the position to Harmon."

"Harmon ran off after you when the battle broke out," Zora points out. "Mother stayed and defended Zechariah."

"Not very well," I mutter. "Since he died and all."

"Mother knows the pack, she knows the laws, she

knows way more than Harmon," Elidi says. "And to be honest, I think she wants it more. Harmon always knew it would be handed to him. Mother's willing to fight for it."

"So is he," I point out. "He's been down here all winter, not off neglecting his duties to be with me, if that's what you're implying."

The whole conversation has irritated me, so I turn away.

"She might seem strict to you, but she's a normal wolf mother," Elidi says at last. "She says she wants to make amends with you. Maybe if you let her, we could...be a family. Now that you don't have Dad..."

I wince at the mention of him, the pain still fresh and raw. After the fire, there was only one funeral. The wolves all got out in time. Only Dad didn't make it. We had a quiet burial in a lot in the shifter valley, where I battled waves of *déjà vous* all night. After all, I'd already gone to one of his funerals, when he faked his death. It made me sad to see how few people showed up, even for their king. He wasn't beloved and popular here. He was a bitter recluse, hated by his people and disinterested in ruling them.

Apparently, not only were our lives better back in Oklahoma, but so were our deaths. His first funeral had tons of his colleagues and friends, people coming by to tell funny stories and bring food. This time, not even Yvonne showed up.

Harmon came with me, and Dr. Golden slipped in a couple minutes after us, her usual long blonde braids hanging at her sides, her eyes red.

A couple of Dad's cousins showed up, along with their

families. I couldn't help staring at them, trying to memorize their faces. The family I never knew existed, still so far removed that I didn't know what to say to them. They kept to themselves, and I didn't want to approach them at a funeral, anyway. But they are there, just over the mountain. I wonder what they're like—savage like Efrain, or quietly malicious like Astrid? Am I like them, a shifty shifter? Are any of them good people?

The last people to arrive were my mother and Elidi. Elidi hung back, looking pale and uncertain. My mother spent the entire time sobbing into a handkerchief.

Now, as I finish pulling nails from the blackened boards, I find myself wondering about her. I haven't seen her much—she's been busy with the wolves like Harmon. This is a test, everyone watching to see how they'll behave in a crisis.

Harmon got the upper hand by finding a place for the wolves to stay and making peace with the witches, however tentative. But I'm sure Mother is cooking up a devious plan to change that.

20

At the end of the day, I put down my tools with the rest of the wolves and witches. I trudge up the mountain, trying not to look at the blackened swath beside us. Behind me, someone says my name, but I don't turn. She repeats it, this time closer, until I have to slow. "Hello, Mother," I say, my voice flat.

"I was hoping we'd have a chance to talk again," she says, falling into step beside me. Today she's wearing dark jeans, tall moccasins, and a slouchy burgundy sweater under a light jacket. Her hair is pulled back in two braids, and her skin has a glow to it that somehow irritates me. Leading half the pack should have made her go gray instead of making her look ten years younger. Harmon looks older, constantly stressed, while Mother looks like she belongs on the pages of a J. Crew catalog. My sisters' words echo in my mind, but I push them away.

"Oh, you mean since the last time, when you threw burning logs at me?" I ask.

"Let's not forget who threw the one that started this," she hisses. "And don't you forget that I know it."

"Thanks, Mother. It's been great talking to you again."

She sighs. "I could tell Harmon, you know."

"Tell him," I say, raising my chin. "You'll find him less than surprised."

"I could tell the others, too," she says, her eyes flashing their usual cruelty. "Once they found out that Harmon already knew, that he still insisted on sticking by his 'Choice,' that would be the end of him."

She sneers at the word "choice," as if it's a mockery. The others hold it so sacred, but I guess after her experience, she sees it as more of a curse than an unbreakable bond.

"You were there that night, too," I remind her. "You're as much to blame as I am. You saw the tree burning, too. Did you stay to watch it spread? Maybe even help it along?"

"But you're the one who threw the flaming torch into the tree," she says with a smirk.

Rage claws its way up my throat, burning when I swallow it back. "You could have stopped it from spreading after I left," I growl.

"Not my responsibility," she says lightly. "The point is, I didn't tell anyone. I could have, and I didn't."

I narrow my eyes at her, remembering what my little outcast group said. Now I'll owe her again. "Thank you, I guess."

"There's no need to thank me," she says with an artificially sweet smile, as if being kind is a challenging endeavor. "I'm your mother. It's my job to protect you, isn't it?"

I choke trying to hold back a laugh.

Mother cuts her eyes at me. "I know I haven't always done a good job," she says. "I'll do better, starting today. Starting with getting you cleaned up. You could really use a haircut, get rid of that damage. And those clothes, my god, you look like a bag lady."

"Great start," I mutter, looking down at the black dress I'm wearing, something Haven apparently stole from the Victorian era. I don't really pay attention to what I look like anymore. It's freeing. I used to spend so much energy on it. Now, I wear anything that fits.

"You're right," Mother says, probably for the first time in her life. "I just hate to see your beauty go to waste. It does get under my skin, but I'll keep my irritation in check. Do you think you could work on that, too? We both have a temper, after all. It runs in the family."

I ignore her ironic smile. If she'd said anything else, I might have thrown it back in her face. But she's right—I'm her daughter. Like it or not, she's the only parent I have left. She and my sisters are still my family, no matter what they believe.

"Here, take this," Mother says, pulling a shiny red apple from the pocket of her belted khaki coat. She offers me a tentative smile. "It's from the batch we picked last fall. I know it's not much, but it's a start, right?"

I hesitate, something inside me recoiling when she reaches out.

"Consider it a peace offering?" She takes my hand and places the apple in my palm, closing my fingers around it. For a moment, she holds my hand in both of hers, and a flash of something like hope flickers across her gaze before it disengages with mine. Quickly, she releases my hand and continues onwards, up the trail we are wearing in the mountainside, just off the burnt section. When we reach the top, I'm a little out of breath. One of the wolves hands me a jar of water, as if I'm just another one of them. As if I'm Elidi.

I take it and drink before passing it along to my mother. Harmon smiles at me from across the circle, where he's talking to one of the warlocks from the First Valley.

"Walk with me to my tent," Mother says. "I have something else for you."

"It's okay," I say, reaching into my pocket and pulling out the apple. "This is enough." I start to lift it to my mouth, but Mother places a hand on my forearm.

"Just wait until you see this," she says, pulling me towards the camp she and her followers have set up, halfway between the lighthouse and the clearing. "I gave you the comb because I want you to think of yourself as part of the family. Yes, family fights sometimes. But they're always there for you."

I cast a glance back at Harmon, wanting to slip over and spend a moment with him. We've all been so busy lately, I've hardly seen him since he came to live up here. But I don't want to interrupt, so I turn and follow my mother.

"I didn't mean you couldn't eat your apple," she says, releasing my arm with an awkward laugh. "Go on, take a bite. They're still crisp, even though it's been months. They keep so well."

"I'm really not hungry," I say, starting to put it into my pocket. But Mother grabs my arm.

"Try it," she says with a tremulous smile, almost begging. "I insist."

"Fine," I say with an irritated sigh. I take a big bite

of it and begin to chew. It really is crisp, and sweet, with not a hint of tartness. It's almost too sweet, with a slight bitterness to the skin, a hint of something like almond. The juice slides down my throat, the sweetness burning. I start to choke, then catch sight of my mother. Her hands are clasped in front of her, and a huge grin spreads across her face, like she's a kid delivering a surprise to her mom on Mother's Day. Not that I know what that looks like.

I try to swallow, to tell her it's a bit much for me. But my voice feels caught, the syrupy juice sliding down my throat but the pulp refusing to follow. I try again, grasping at my throat.

"It's time," Mother cries ecstatically at the sky.

Still trying to cough out the offending bite, I bend forward. Blackness swims in my vision, and I sink to my knees. I can't swallow the apple. I can't cough it out.

"I'll push her out while she's weak," Mother says, her voice sounding different somehow, harsher, less southern. I tumble into the leaves. Bare branches swim against the deep blue of the evening sky. I focus on the one star visible.

Someone else slips between the trees, a shadowy figure moving in the corner of my vision. Long auburn hair. Bare skin.

"As soon as she leaves her body, I'll take it over. You bind her into a tree before she can turn into one of those screaming wraiths and drive me mad."

"Yes, Mother Dear," Astrid says, her eyes cast down. She bends over me, as if checking for breath.

Mother. Astrid called her *mother.*

A shock wave of fury and betrayal rocks through my body. Astrid told me that Yvonne was her *mother dear*.

Yvonne is her mother.

Suddenly, all the strangeness of my mother's visits flashes through my wavering mind. Her clothes. Her contradictions. That screechy laugh. Her rage when I wouldn't project, even though it had killed her father. The odd mannerisms. Mannerisms that aren't my mother's at all. They are Yvonne's, Mrs. Nguyen's, the sorceress's.

It wasn't my mother. My mother would never ask to be my friend. She'd never give me gifts. She hates projection. She'd never ask me to do that. She probably never told me because she hoped I'd never find out I could do it. How could I have been so blind? It was someone else all along. Someone who knows how to project.

Doralice's words whisper in my mind. *Beware the mirror.*

I was warned. Mother warned me before she became the mirror. Why didn't I listen?

After checking my pulse, Astrid begins to sit back on her heels, but before she straightens, her eyes lock on mine. She mouths a single word, "Go."

I let my eyes fall closed as my consciousness threatens to leave me. And I remember all that I've learned about projecting—if someone is pushed from their body, or the stronger spirit refuses to relinquish its grasp on a body, the true owner of the body is killed. If she pushes me out, I won't be able to come back. But if I go voluntarily, I can creep back in, can't I? When she's sleeping, or not acting as my mirror. When she abandons my body to go inhabit another. If I'm not dead, I won't be a ghost, exactly, but a wandering spirit.

But I've never projected in my life. I don't know how.

Do I?

I think of what she told me. Of what Dad told me. Everything I know. The leaves crunch beside me as my mother's body falls, empty and abandoned. Discarded.

Something jerks at my consciousness. The feeling is abhorrent, repulsive. Everything in me screams at me to fight it, to push back as Yvonne tries to enter my body. But there is not much left in me. Already, I feel far away from my body. I picture myself shooting up, out of my body. I picture myself blazing through the cold twilight like a swimmer shooting up towards the surface of the water. A shooting star in a constellation, my namesake. Heading for the only other star in the sky, the evening star high above.

As darkness closes in, a pulse of fear clenches inside me, like the moment before you jump from a high-dive. But I can also feel Yvonne struggling to gain access to my body. So with a final release, I wrench myself away and let go.

21

I fly, untethered by my body or the earth, for a second that is also eternity. And then, as quickly as I was free, I am bound. I stop short, like a dog that's run full speed until it reaches the end of its chain. I am yanked back.

From somewhere far away, voices invade my consciousness. I reel back towards earth, towards the body I left. I can feel it calling, pulling, as if I'm a rubber band that has been pulled taut. Terrified to have left my body abandoned, for the taking, I hurtle back. And then, I catch on something familiar, a chant in a voice I know. Haven's voice mingles with Astrid's, flowing over and then under it, both speaking rapidly as if racing to finish first.

With a start, I'm deposited back in the world of the living. Except I can't see anything. I can't exactly hear, and yet, I know and understand the words being spoken nearby, as if I am absorbing them through my skin. If I have skin.

"Done," Astrid says, her voice slumping with exhaustion.

"Me, too," Haven says smugly, just seconds later.

Is she in on this? Rage swells inside me, and I try to move, to sit up, but I can't. I am frozen, solid and still. Panic swells in my chest, and I try again, but I can't break free. I concentrate, trying to throw myself upwards again, but I am held fast. Is this how my tiger felt all those years, trapped inside my body by an enchanted necklace, unable to move? I want to scream, but I have no voice, no mouth.

But someone else is screaming. A familiar voice screeches, "What have you done? I can't enter her body!"

"Oh, Auntie," Haven says. "You taught me well."

If I had lungs, I'd suck in a breath. If I had lungs, I'd scream.

"You bitch," my mother's voice shrieks. But it's not really her voice, not really my mother.

"That's me," Haven says, sound unconcerned. "In fact, I thought that was your cute nickname for me until I was like, eight."

"You did this," Yvonne snarls. "Now undo it! As your elder, I command you."

"All those years of protecting your body while you were gone, of learning the spells to keep others from possessing whatever body you dragged home. You didn't think I'd forget them, did you? Oh, I guess you probably would, though. Considering I'm so useless, and untalented, and blah blah blah."

"This will be the last time," Yvonne promises, her voice wheedling. "I swear to you both, I won't waste this one. I can be Stella. With a handsome husband who loves me, the leader of the Three Valleys. That's what everyone wants. All the creatures united under one leader. I am what they want, what they need. Just let me have her."

"Yeah, I'm going to have to say no," Haven says. "No matter how young or beautiful or powerful you are, you'll never be satisfied."

"You will pay for this!" Yvonne shrieks.

143

"I don't know," Haven says. "You already tried to steal my body, but you couldn't push me out. Remember? And since I have no talent for projection, you can't steal it the way you're trying to steal Stella's now."

"But I need this," Yvonne says, her voice edging back from hysteria towards desperation. "You don't know what it's like to spend your whole life jumping from one body to the next, always hoping you'll find one that's good enough to make you forget that it doesn't belong to you. You don't know what it's like to go through life knowing you're in the wrong body, to feel it like a panic crawling up your back, hanging there no matter how you try to shake it off, to forget it."

"Yeah, that's sad," Haven says. "But so is killing all those people, just to use their bodies and dispose of them like garbage when you get tired of them."

"It's like an itch that never goes away, that drives me mad from within," Yvonne rants. "Make it stop!"

"Help her," Astrid says. "What do you care whose body she takes, as long as it's not yours?"

"Maybe next time, it will be," Haven says. "It could be mine, or yours, or anyone's. She'll never stop. And she gets stronger every time she does it. What if she gets so strong she can steal it from someone when they're conscious? She'll be unstoppable."

"I'll stop," Yvonne moans. "I promise. Just let me have Stella. She doesn't even take care of it! Look at that youth, that beauty, wasted."

"You have a new body," Haven says. "You've only been in that one for—what? A month? Two or three? You killed that woman for a month's stay in her body? That's disgusting."

"I needed it," Yvonne roars. "It was all part of the plan, leading up to this moment. I've been waiting for this moment since the day she was born. I should have gotten her instead of this useless floozy."

"Me?" Astrid protests, sounding wounded.

"Yes, you," Yvonne snaps. In my mother's mouth, those words sound so familiar, like it's really her. But she's gone. Dead. She's been gone for months, even before Dad. I'm an orphan, and I didn't even know it. The connections between us tangle my brain. It would give me a headache if I had a head.

Instead, I have branches, roots, and bark. I can feel the leaves budding inside me, waiting to burst forth and unfurl. At the same time, I can feel the ache in my nonexistent gut at the news of my mother's death. She was so far from perfect it's not even funny. Maybe I should hate her. And yet…she was still my mother. Like with my father, I can't hold onto resentment when she's gone. There are still so many questions inside me that I never got to ask. But those stories died when she died.

"If you won't let me have her, she's as good as dead," Yvonne says. "Astrid has trapped her inside a tree, and you'll never know which one. By the time it dies, her body will have wasted away. It could be centuries."

"She's my friend," Haven says. "And I'm not giving you her body so you can possess her like the demon you are."

Yvonne shrieks, and I am aware of their scuffle. My limbs tremble with the unbearable urge to jump in, to defend Haven and fight by her side. But my feet are literally planted in the ground. A scream bubbles up inside me, but it only festers there, building pressure that cannot be released. It's maddening, like Yvonne described her itch to find the right body. I can't help my friend, even after, somehow, she sealed my body from Yvonne's invasion.

At last, Yvonne speaks, panting and out of breath. "Take her to the tower," she says. "Let's see how she likes being trapped and helpless."

The scream wells inside me. They haven't killed Haven —I can still feel her life force, her presence nearby. But she's incapacitated, maybe unconscious. At least Yvonne isn't ripping her soul from her body and acting as her mirror.

"How am I supposed to get her up there?" Astrid asks. Compared to Haven, she's waifish and small. I wonder if there is a door somewhere after all, one that Yvonne is about to reveal.

Instead, she says, "You'll figure it out."

"Where are you going?" Astrid asks, sounding like a little girl being left alone in the woods.

"I'm taking Stella to the wolves," she says. "I'll tell them she's dead. Harmon has already Chosen her, but once his mate is dead, he can marry someone else. It won't matter. He might not love you, but you'll be his wife."

"Me?" Astrid squeaks.

"Yes, you dolt," Yvonne snaps. "Now get that body hidden."

"I don't want to marry a wolf. They're scary."

"What does it matter? You're a witch, you can have a whole collective of husbands. And you're the rightful heir to the shifter throne. Harmon will marry you to unite the valleys. If he can't have his mate, he'll at least make an advantageous, loveless marriage. I'll step down from challenging him as I mourn my daughter. And all will be as it should."

"You won't...try to take my place? Because you said that exact same thing about Stella. And now she's as good as dead."

"Because she didn't succeed," Yvonne says. "You, my dear, will. You did as I asked at every turn, haven't you? Unlike the others, you have not betrayed me. As long as you stay as obedient to me as you are now, no harm will come to you when you are queen."

After a moment, Astrid speaks, her soft voice barely more than a whisper. "Yes, Mother Dear."

I want to scream as they move away. To warn Astrid, despite all she's done. Because she may have done what Yvonne wanted, but she also betrayed her. Maybe it was a small betrayal, telling me to leave my body instead of waiting for her mother to kill me before trapping me in the tree. But I have a feeling if Yvonne knew, she wouldn't care how small the betrayal. I can only imagine what she did to Haven, and my nonexistent heart cries for the sacrifice she made for me.

22

As time passes, how long I cannot tell, I realize the horror of my situation. I am here, but no one knows. At first, I only notice the people. They walk by, talking and laughing, bickering and silent. Wolf people pass my tree daily on their way to and from their camp. I want to scream, to kick and flail and wail, to have a tantrum. But I am entombed in this tree, like a fly in amber.

And then one day, the talking multiplies. Everyone is chattering, and there is lots of activity under my branches as people pass back and forth. I hear my sisters. I hear Harmon. That's when I know. Harmon is at my mother's camp, helping them move. They are all packing up and leaving. The pack has been reunited.

A wall of emotion hits me so hard I think I'll expire, that the tree I'm inhabiting will wither and die. I send out a wave of energy like a shockwave across the valley, willing him to recognize me. To know that I'm still here.

But he doesn't hear me. He can't. He is gone now, carrying a load down the path. Does this mean he's married Astrid, whom he doesn't love and who doesn't love him?

It hits me again, the true horror of this trap. He might marry her, and I'll never know. And why shouldn't he? He's stuck forever alone even in marriage, forever without being able to give or receive real love. But at least he'll have companionship if he marries Astrid. Maybe he'll even have children. He can love them as a father. I'm sure he'll make a great leader and a great father, as he wants to be. Once, he told me he wanted a big family. I wonder if Astrid wants that, and how it even works, if she has many husbands.

I have lots of time to remember. Each day is an eternity in the forest, as I silently scream myself towards insanity. The wolves trickle away, and the forest is silent.

Rain falls, but I am not cold. The sun beats down, but I am not hot. I am alone.

But a while after the humans leave, I begin to hear other sounds. The softer sounds of the forest. An ant crawling up my bark. A mole burrowing beneath my roots. Birds flitting between my branches. The sigh of the wind, always carrying whispers.

At first, I think I really have gone insane. I'm hearing voices. Whispery voices that touch whatever part of me is still aware enough to absorb conversations though I do not have ears to hear. Though I hadn't noticed them, they suddenly wash over me like a wave of insect song in summer. They've been there all along, background noise, that I only now recognize when human voices are gone, when I have nothing to cut me through with longing.

"—guess it is my just desserts—"

"—didn't know it would last so long—"

"—wish I'd been on the mountainside that burned—"

"—at least we're still—"

"—seen my granddaughter in a hundred years—"

I'm jolted back from my misery. I can feel them all

around me now, spreading out for miles. We are all part of this tapestry, this forest. Not all the trees have ghosts in them. Most of them are just trees. But I can feel the ones that do, the different energy of the ones with human souls.

"Who's out there?" I ask, sending out the thought in hopes someone will hear it.

"The new one speaks," someone says, with humor in her voice.

"We got a newcomer!" another voice says.

I'm reminded, with a pang, of Xela's excitement when I joined them. I hope she's safe from Yvonne, wherever she is. I hope that Haven has returned to her collective.

"Are you witches?" I ask.

"Goodness, no, child," a voice answers. "We're tree spirits."

"Or ghosts, if you prefer," another says.

"But what were you before?" I ask.

A long silence. "I'm not sure," one answers.

"After a while, it doesn't matter," another adds. "This is who we are. Everyone's the same when you're a ghost. Doesn't matter what size or shape you were. You're just a ghost."

Yvonne's words clatter through my mind, her search for the right body. Maybe this is what she needs—to not have one.

"An angry ghost, right?" I ask.

Laughter dances through the leaves on the trees. I can't remember how long I've had leaves, but I have them, too. "Oh, no," one says. "Anger doesn't last long. It isn't real."

"Try telling that to the new ones, though, and they never understand," another says. "Once you've been in the spirit world a while, it goes away. Some people wish they could get out and move on, but most of us don't mind staying between the spirit and physical world. We can see our families grow, or hear about it. When a person passes by, we pass along the news. Somewhere, someone is waiting for it."

"What about the angry wraiths?"

"Oh, that's just the new ones," one says. "We got one recently. Won't even talk yet. Refuses to join in with us."

"Is my father here?" I ask hopefully. For a while, there is just the whisper of the wind through the trees, the sigh of their voices. But eventually, the news comes back.

"No one thinks he is," an answer comes. "Was he angry when he died? Vengeful? Was he murdered?"

"No," I admit. "Holding onto his petty prejudices about werewolves, but that's about it. I don't think he was actually angry."

"Then he passed on peacefully into the spirit world. That's okay, too."

"Even better," another voice says.

"So how do I get out of here?" I ask.

"Oh, child," a ghost says. "You don't."

"Not until your tree dies."

"And you seem young and healthy."

"But you can watch your children grow, then your grandchildren. Maybe even great grandchildren."

"I don't have kids."

"No kids?"

"Such a shame."

"I'm not dead," I say. "I was put here by a spell."

"Same as the rest of us," says a ghost.

"Yeah, but we were bothering the living world," says another. "This was our punishment for haunting."

"There's nothing I can do?"

"If a person touches you, you can sometimes speak with them," a ghost says.

"You can always talk to us," says another. "And to other ghosts as they pass on. That way, you'll know who enters the forest, and who goes on to the spirit world."

"What about my mother?" I ask. "She's pretty much the definition of angry and vengeful. Is she here?"

Another long pause while the message goes through the forest. The answer comes back eventually. "I think she's the newcomer who won't talk to us," a ghost says.

"Figures," I answer. "Whoever is near her, please tell her that her daughter is stuck here, and I'd like to talk to her when she feels like it."

"She can hear you," the ghost says. "We can all hear each other."

Great. So she just heard everything I said.

Life as a tree spirit wouldn't be too bad, maybe, if I was already dead and the alternative was to just vanish into the spirit world. The ghosts have tons of stories, and despite what the wolves believe, most of them are not angry. They're mischievous, and will snatch up unsuspecting humans to have a laugh about it. But they rarely carry any malice. Mostly, they tell stories and gossip like they're at a quilting bee instead of trapped in a secluded forest. The thing is, they're not alone. They're all together, and they treat me like one of them, even though I'm not.

Whenever I feel myself slipping into their routine, though, becoming one of them, I remind myself fiercely that I'm not. That I will get out. But as the weeks pass, it becomes harder and harder to believe.

Until one night, when the moon is full, I hear howling so close it almost makes my bark tremble. I can feel the vibration of the lonesome, mournful howl all the way through me, from my roots to my topmost leaves. It's Harmon. I can't see him, but I know. My heart knows, and it cracks for him, though he can't see me, either. He can't see that this is me, that I wish I could let his cry split my trunk as if struck by lightning. That's how it feels.

I reach for him, only now beginning to control the motion of my branches. The effort exhausts me, but I stretch towards him. If only I can touch him, let him know I'm still here. But he races off, the motion so close to my leaves that I'm left swaying in his wake. I want to scream again, to laugh in the maniacal way Yvonne does. I know what it's like to be trapped in the wrong body. Oh, I understand that, all right. The difference is, I didn't choose to be here, in this tree. I didn't kill this tree and steal its form.

Rage races through me, along my branches and over my leaves. But I am stuck, unable to move. When I was trapped in Mother's attic, at least I could hope. When I was trapped in Harmon's basement, at least I could read, talk to him, formulate a plan. Even being trapped as a human when I wanted to be a tiger was bearable. This—this is not. I remember reading *Dante's Inferno* on the long days in Harmon's basement. And I think now that Dante had it right—the worst circle of hell, the worst torture, is being stuck.

Something brushes against my leaves, the branch still outstretched to touch Harmon. The wolf lets out a cry as if in pain, and I recoil. But the wolf stays, whining on the ground beneath my branches. Another wolf joins him, and for a while, they remain there, communicating silently in some language I never understood and so cannot now. At last, they change into human form. The moment they are in human form, I recognize them as if I have sight again. Fernando and Zora.

It could be worse.

"Who are you?" Fernando asks, but it's Zora who reaches out and touches me.

She spreads her palm flat against my bark, and I can feel the defiance rolling off her.

"Stella," I say, as urgently as I can, hoping it will convey to a language she can understand. In all the days I've been part of this ghostly forest, days that blur together into weeks and now months, I've never asked how to speak to humans. I've never asked if it takes practice, if I'll have to learn a new language.

Zora gasps and pulls her hand back. "It's Stella."

I guess that's a no on the new language.

"Are you sure?" Fernando asks.

"I'm sure," she says, her voice ringing with excitement. I admit, that's the last thing I expected from Zora. I was hoping I could convince her, maybe even bribe her, to tell someone about me. Bargaining has always gotten me what I want with Zora, but this time, she offers no resistance or resentment. "Wait until we tell the others," she says. "Let's mark her and go tell them."

"You're going to pee on your sister?" Fernando asks.

"Good point," Zora says. "Let me find a rock and I'll chip off some of her bark. And maybe pee on her just a little. She deserves it."

There's the Zora I know and, right now, completely love. I don't even care that she's marking my tree like I'm her territory.

When they've marked me, they shift back to wolves and run off to join the pack further down the valley. I can feel them better than I could as a human, through the other trees, the other ghosts. I wait, so relieved I want to melt. All night, I wait, and wait, and wait. It feels like a hundred years. But no one comes for me.

By morning, I realize they're not coming.

23

Somehow, I misread Zora's excitement. Or maybe she told the woman she thinks is her mother, and Yvonne told her not to tell anyone. For all I know, she killed Zora to keep her silent. It seems she has no qualms about murder when it suits her purposes.

Or maybe she told Harmon, and he didn't believe her. I know how crazy it sounds. "By the way, I ran into your mate in the forest last night. Oh yeah, and she's a tree."

I won't let myself consider the other option. That he's already married, and it's too painful to come up here and be devastated all over again, knowing that it's too late. I won't let myself hope. Because if Zora told Yvonne, she won't just silence Zora. She'll find a way to get rid of me. She'll be furious that I reached out, that I tried to communicate with someone. Tried to get free.

And what happened to my body? Yvonne herself told me the dangers of projecting. She told me what could happen to a body. If she told Harmon I was dead, and he buried my body, it's probably nothing but a skeleton by now.

Or, if I'm super-duper lucky, I haven't decomposed quite so far. I could come back as a reanimated corpse, because everyone wants a zombie for a bride.

I've given up hope when I hear the rustling of the trees, excitement building as they relay a message. Someone is coming, a human is coming. Does it belong to anyone here?

I try to quash my hopes, knowing it could be anyone. And then he is there, standing beneath my branches. My soul, my mate.

He clears his throat, uncertainty rolling off him in waves. "I don't know how this works," he mutters. "Is this you?"

I reach for him, stretching my limbs, my leaves aching for a touch. He tenses, but after a moment, his fingers stretch towards me, tentative and a bit afraid. "It's me," I say, sending the message with all my strength.

Harmon sucks in a breath. "Stella? Is it really you?" His voice breaks with emotion, but he quickly recovers himself. "Does this mean you're dead?"

"I'm here." My vocabulary seems limited, my ability to speak muddled. Now I know why Doralice couldn't have a conversation. There are only simple phrases, not all the small uncertainties and filler words I want to use.

I don't know if I'm dead. I don't know how this works. If I leave this tree, will I pass into the spirit world? Did my body die while I was here? How would I know?

"How do I get you out?" he asks. While I'm stuck in frustration, he is already moving ahead, looking for solutions.

"Set me free," I whisper to him through my leaves, a feeling more than words.

"How?" he asks, his own frustration coming through.

"Cut down the tree."

He's quiet a long moment. "What if it kills you?"

I want to tell him I'll take the chance, that this is death anyway. I want to tell him some of the ghosts long for death, long to be free. But all I can do is repeat the same instruction. *Cut me down.*

"I don't know if I can," he says quietly. "Not if it might kill you. If I know you're here, I can visit." He breaks off for a moment, his fingers caressing my leaves. "But I guess that's not fair to you. To keep you trapped here, like an animal in a zoo, so I can come and see you, talk to you. You're not a headstone."

His words cut deep, into my core. He gave me up for dead. He's grieved me, maybe is still grieving. To him, I was gone. Does that mean he's moved on, has taken over the pack, has united with Astrid, the shifter queen? I can't ask these things yet, until I have a voice and can formulate the words I want to say.

"I'll come back for you," he says. His voice sounds older, wearied. And then he is gone.

The trees mutter and whisper, ask me questions. But for once, I am too despondent to respond. Though I can talk to them, communicate fully in the language of ghosts, I have nothing to say.

I wait again. All this waiting. It's good the ghosts have each other, or they'd surely go insane from the waiting, the endless passage of time, the changelessness of the changing seasons.

And then one voice cuts through the other ghost voices, a voice I know well, a presence I loathe and fear and long for at once. "Stella. My daughter."

I draw up instinctively, putting up a layer of protection around myself.

"You're going home," Mother says—my real mother, Talia. Not Yvonne. "You can still do that, you have a body. You were not torn free as I was."

"Lucky me."

"She put you here, didn't she? That witch. That sorceress, the queen of the mirror. You're not the first she's done this to. Only the first who escaped."

"I don't know if I'd call it escape," I say. "I'm here in the forest, locked inside a tree like the rest of you."

"Not like the rest of us," she says fiercely. "You have a second chance to live, Stella."

"I'm beginning to think it's not much better than being a ghost."

"You're wrong. You may never understand, but Yvonne ruined my life long before she took it."

"So Yvonne killed you. She snatched your body and became your mirror. And she's living your life."

"Not for the first time. Last time, I had the protection of a curse. A loophole. But this time, she crept in while I was sleeping. When I wasn't expecting it and could not keep her from invading. A thief in the night."

"That sucks, Mom. It really does. I'm sorry."

She's quiet a long time. "I made mistakes," she says. "I always knew that one day, they'd catch up to me. I suspect she has been visiting me for a while now. I'd wake in the morning as tired as when I went to sleep. Things didn't feel right. But the last time...when I tried to wake, she held on tighter. I couldn't push her out. The bond between myself and my body was torn. Maybe it was because I'd left my body before, and the bond that held me to it was never the same. Maybe I had been waiting my whole life for her to come back and claim my body again. Or maybe, in some way, I knew I deserved it. But you don't."

"I did the same to your father." Being here, in this forest, connected to all the trees and the ghosts, has done something to me. Like they said, it's hard to hold on to anger as a tree. I don't even hate my mother anymore. She tried to warn me about Yvonne. That was still her. The next time I saw her, she was someone else. The mirror. The sorceress.

"You were a tool of your own father's," Talia says after a while.

"For once, we're in agreement." How could I have known what would happen, when I was three years old? Still, guilt seeps through me. Maybe I deserve it, too.

"I know that you don't owe me anything," she says. "But I want you to do something for me, if you can."

"Okay…"

"You need to kill Yvonne."

"About that…"

"No one will be safe with the sorceress here. She's the only one powerful enough to project the way she does. Now that your father is gone, there's only two people who can do what you can do. There's you, and there's her. And she won't stop as long as she knows that."

The trees sigh and whisper, gossiping about my mother's broken silence, about our conversation, about whether Harmon will return.

"I'll think about it," I say.

"I hope you do. Because if it were up to her, you'd be

here forever. And she'd be living your life, lying with your mate, raising your children, enjoying your freedom. As you, not me. And no one would ever know it wasn't you. She's not your babysitter. She's an evil enchantress. And as soon as you are back, she'll try again. She'll never stop trying, until you're dead."

"Okay, okay. I got it."

"I mean it, Stella. I may not have been good or fair to you. But I did try to protect you. So I'm going to try one more time. Her time was over a long time ago. She's kept living by taking the lives of others. They were not hers to take. And she'll stop at nothing to have more power, more beauty. Harmon won't be safe. Your children won't be safe. I speak from experience. This experience, seeing my child in this forest."

Did she just call me her child? Part of me still twists when she says it. For so long, I wanted that more than anything. A family, somewhere to belong.

But it's too little too late.

"May you have the strength to face her," she says. "Remember, Stella. You are not only a girl. You are a tigress. A mighty hunter. It is in your nature to kill, just as it is in your nature to love Harmon, to want what is yours."

What is mine. My body, my life. Harmon. A family. But it won't include her.

At last, I feel a pull like no other, a need full of pain and longing and desire and love. Harmon is coming back for me. My soul swells with hope, with overwhelming gratitude and joy.

"Mother," I say, before it's too late. "Do you want me

to do the same for you? Do you want me to come back and cut down your tree? I can free you."

She's silent a long moment, so long I think she's ignoring me again. But at last she speaks, just as Harmon reaches me. "No," she says. "But maybe someday, when you have fulfilled your purpose, when all the peoples of the Three Valleys can pass without notice from one valley to the next, when everyone lives in harmony and there is no danger in it…maybe you can bring your children here to play."

She doesn't say more, doesn't beg, doesn't grovel for my promise. She doesn't say they need to play under her tree, or that I should tell them about her. That is not my mother. She may not apologize and offer phony peace offerings or ask to be my friend. But I can live with that.

"I'll do that," I say. I will do a million things if I can just be human again. Forgive my father for keeping the truth from me. I'll never know how my life would have been if I'd known who I was all my life. But the truth is, those years of not knowing were happy years.

I'll forgive my mother. She was cruel, but life made her that way.

I'll take care of that human body I took for granted, that I scorned because my tiger form was so superior. Now I'd give anything to be a weak, clumsy human. I'll take care of my human side, cut my hair, find a middle ground between the beauty-obsessed kid I was when I arrived in the Second Valley and the slob I was when I left it.

I'll forgive the wolves for their fear of me. I won't let my own fear of them keep me from the one I love more than anyone. I'll accept my sisters as family, because they are the family I have left. I will do so many things I should have done before, if only I can get my human body back. This tree is no place for a human soul. All I want is to be free of it.

Until the ax bites into my flesh.

24

Pain shrieks through me, through every fiber of my being. Through my bark and trunk, my branches and twigs, my leaves. Through the tree that I am, because this is my body. It travels inwards, spiraling towards my soul, residing here.

"I'm sorry," Harmon says, his voice ragged. "I can't do this. I can feel how much it hurts you."

After a moment, I force the silent screams to calm, to form into words. I force them through every screaming inch of my tree. "Keep going."

He must hear the determination in my words, because he pulls the ax free and swings again. Pain washes through me. My pain. His pain. The horror of what he's doing. The chance that it won't work, that he's killing his mate. That I'm asking him to.

The blade slices through my flesh again, and again, and again. I scream with each blow, but when he stops to swipe the sweat from his brow, his breath coming in quick, jerky gasps, I tell him to go on.

The forest with all its ghosts pays silent witness to my torment. I am voiceless, soundless, sightless. Nothing but a lightning rod of agony, silently screaming as the ax bites into my flesh. It is blinding, insanity-inducing pain, ripping through me with each strike as it conquers my outer walls, my bark, into the softer flesh. He swings again, and the ax slices deeper into me. I won't stop him.

The moment the last fiber of wood splits from the stump, before the weight of the top half begins to fall, I am hurtling from the tree with a shriek that contains all the things I could not express. The depths of pain I never knew existed, the anger and frustration and fury and help-lessness—all of it comes out in one earth shattering shriek, like a sonic boom as I snap back towards my body at the speed of light. I hit with the force of a lightning bolt.

The force of the blow stuns me senseless for a moment. It's like I've hit a wall made of the finest, clearest quartz, one that I can't see even with my inner eyes, my sightless new knowing. At first, I think I've been thrown backwards by the blow, that I'm tumbling away into space. But then I sense the shattering of the crystal, the frag-ments splintering and flying in every direction like shrapnel as I blast through a barrier, back into me.

The grinding, shrieking squeal of the crystal plates raking across each other punctures my eardrums with its ferocity. I scream again, trying to clutch at my ears.

And suddenly, I can.

I'm back in a body of substance, heavy and warm again, my hands clumsy as I reach for my ears. Choking, I lean over, and a single piece of apple falls from my lips. Something so small, seemingly so benign as a bite of apple, still white with a bit of shiny red skin, almost killed me. Lying back, I blink dumbly at the sky, the trees above, the boy bending over me. All of it is so bright, blindingly real and solid.

"Is it really you, Stella?" Harmon looks ten years older

than the last time I saw him, with the finest lines at the corners of his eyes. His cheeks are wet, but he's laughing, too, pulling my body into his lap and smiling down at me. He brought me my body, laid it at my feet.

"It's me," I whisper.

"You better not ever leave me like that again," he says. "That's a direct order from your Alpha."

"I'm not a wolf," I say, my voice a strange croak. My face feels strange when I smile, like I've gone to the dentist and I'm completely numb. I just know my face is doing something totally weird that I didn't tell it to do.

"I don't care," he growls. "It's still an order."

"You don't get to order me around. I'm bigger than you," I remind him.

"I have a whole pack at my disposal," he says. "You're only one tiger."

And then he's laughing, wiping his cheeks, his lips finding mine. Heat rises in my core, bringing me back to life, reminding me what it feels like to have blood in my veins, heat in my body. My arms twine around his neck, and the relief of being able to move my limbs at will engulfs me as I embrace him. My fingers sink into his thick hair, my mouth hungry for his mouth, my body hungry for his body. I tear at his clothes, desperate to feel human again, to enjoy this human body in a way I haven't since finding out I was a shifter.

Sure, being a tiger is great. But this—this is what it feels like to be truly alive.

25

When we've finished with our reunion, Harmon dresses in silence. I'm still not used to this whole sleeping-together thing, since we've only done it the one time, so I dress with my back to him, trying not to analyze his behavior. Still, when I finish and we both stand, I have to clear my throat to rid myself of the awkward tension.

"So…are you married now?" I ask.

Harmon rocks back like I just punched him in the chest. "What?"

"Well, you know. Mrs.—Yvonne. She said you could marry Astrid if I was dead, and you thought I was dead, so…"

"Stop," Harmon says. He steps over to me and cups my face between his hands, tilting my face up to his so I have to meet his eyes. "I told you. That's not how it works. There is no one but you, and there never will be. I will keep telling you that until you believe me."

"I'm sorry," I say, pulling away. "I just thought…we haven't had the mating ceremony anyway, and you've had girlfriends before…"

"Everything before we Choose a mate is kid's stuff," he says, taking both my hands. "Yes, we live close, people get crushes, they have girlfriends and boyfriends, but it's not serious. It's not this." He squeezes my hands. "I would have waited for you to wake up until the day I died."

"Sorry," I say again, shaking my head. "I do know. It was hard living apart from you, and Yvonne put ideas in my head...of course she's the one who can't be trusted. Not you." I slide my arms around him and rest my cheek against his chest. His strong arms encircle my body, and he rests his cheek on top of my head. For a long while, neither of us move.

At last, he pulls away, his eyes serious. "This has gone on long enough," he says. "It's time to do something about your mother."

So much has happened that it takes me a moment to realize he's not talking about my mother, the tree. He still thinks Yvonne is my mother.

"She's not my mother," I tell him. And then I tell him everything else. It's a relief to speak again after so long, and it all comes pouring out—her strange behavior when she visited, how she didn't act like herself. A growl builds low in Harmon's throat when I tell him about the fight I had with her the day of the fire. But when I tell him about her trying to take my body, his blue eyes harden into deadly blades of ice.

A realization jars me out of my story. "Haven," I cry. "We need to get Haven."

"Okay..." Harmon says. "That's the wild witch, right?"

"Yes," I say, already starting towards the clearing. "Come on, hurry."

As we make our way there, it's Harmon's turn to fill

me in on events. After I was put into the tree that night, Talia—or Yvonne, dressed in Talia's body—sneaked my body into my nest, where Harmon found it the next morning.

I try not to think about what he went through, but I know what it's like to find the body of someone you love. I raise his hand to my lips and kiss his knuckles as we walk.

My mother, or the woman Harmon thought was my mother, pretended to be devastated, and kept saying she wanted to bury me and get it over with, that she couldn't bear the pain of having my body around. This aroused Harmon's suspicions, and he contacted Dr. Golden without my mother's knowledge. When she found out, she was furious and tried to stop Dr. Golden from disturbing my body, which only made Harmon more determined. At that point, he thought I was dead and that my mother must have poisoned me.

Dr. Golden told him that I was alive, but I had been put to sleep by some kind of potion. Unfortunately, without a sample, Dr. Golden couldn't tell what was in it or what could counter it. Fortunately, my body had also been put under some kind of protection spell that would keep evil spirits away and preserve it until I woke.

"Haven did that," I say, increasing my pace until I'm almost running. I'm still wearing my clothes from last winter, and they seem to weigh me down in the humid summer air. But I barely feel the heat trapped inside the black dress—one of Haven's—and the sweat gathering on my skin. All I can think about is that she saved my life, and it might have cost her own.

Harmon says that once the houses were fixed up enough to go back, the wolves moved back down into the valley. The only house that was completely lost was his. He doesn't make a big deal about it, but I can see the pain etched into his face. He lost his father this year, too, and his home. And me.

I glance around at the trees of the Enchanted Forest. Though I wonder what the ghosts are saying around me, I can't hear them anymore. I can only hear the cacophony of crickets and cicadas and katydids, and the steady murmur of Harmon's voice.

I'm surprised to hear that when the pack found out I'd been put under a spell, they were outraged and wanted to protect me. Unfortunately, the situation also kindled their old distrust of the witches, and they moved off the mountain. Mother tried to say it was Harmon's fault, since he'd pushed for alliance with the witches, but anyone could see he would never intentionally do anything to endanger me.

When Dr. Golden told him I was alive, he carried my body with him down the mountain, to the new house the community built for us, this one just a simple cabin like the rest.

"I read to you sometimes," he says, shooting me an uncertain look. "I know you like Shakespeare. I didn't know if you could hear me."

"Aww," I say, and watch color climb into his cheeks.

"I thought you were in there somewhere," he explains. "Like a coma."

"What about Mother? What was she doing all this time?"

"She was pushing me to marry the new shifter heir,"

he says, cutting his eyes sideways at me. "She actually lost some support among the wolves for it, but it didn't seem to bother her. Now I know why."

"She's invested in both sides," I say. "She wins either way. Either she's Alpha, or her daughter is married to the Alpha."

"Unless we kill her."

I suck in a breath at the callous, almost casual way he says it. But then I remember that death is not a shocking concept to them. It shouldn't be to me, either. For wolves and shifters, death is part of life. I've been exclusively human for too long, growing up never knowing that was part of my heritage. But if I'm going to be a shifter, or an honorary wolf who can't shift, I should get used to their way of life.

"I'm going to kill her," Harmon says solemnly. "Are you okay with that? I know she's your mother, but—."

"She's not my mother," I cut in sharply.

"She has your mother's body. Will it be hard for you to know I did that?"

"No," I say, my voice colder than I've ever heard it.

We pass one of the camps where the wolves stayed, the leaves still crushed down and paths still worn into the ground. And then we reach the hive, and beyond it, the clearing where Doralice once stood. When we draw near, I hear voices, laughter. It strikes me as strange, suddenly, how normal everything sounds. Life really does go on, is always going on, all around us.

I brush my fingers against a tree trunk and smile as we step into the clearing.

For a second, no one notices. Then a piercing shriek

splits the air, and a sturdy little blonde elf charges me. I catch her in my arms, my breath knocked out, and Harmon catches us both so we don't go sprawling. I'm going to have to learn to plant my feet in preparation for Xela's hugs.

"You're back," she crows. "You guys, Stella's back. We haven't seen you since that night you disappeared with Haven. At first we thought maybe she'd finally worn you down and gotten you to join her collective, ran off on a honeymoon. Then they found your body the next day, and Haven never came back..." She breaks off, her eyes moistening.

My heart thuds painfully in my chest. "Haven never came back?"

"No," Uzula says, slinking across the clearing to join us. "We looked everywhere."

"We were hoping you could tell us what happened to her when you woke up. And here you are!" Xela throws her arms up, then lowers them and gives me a mischievous wink, peering past me to Harmon. "And you brought me something pretty!"

"Very funny," Harmon says, but he's smiling.

Xela's smile falters. "You don't know where Haven is?"

I swallow the sour taste in the back of my throat. "The last I heard, Yvonne ordered Astrid to put her in the tower."

"What are we waiting for?" Kale asks, leaping across the clearing in one bound, landing in a crouch. "Let's go get her."

Together, we all traipse back through the forest—an Alpha wolf without his title, a shifter who can't shift, a faerie who lost his love, a friendly elf, a surly troll, and Uzula, of mysterious origins. When we get to the briar patch around the lighthouse, Xela groans and Yorn grumbles. Kale studies it silently, then crouches. The next moment, he's twenty feet away, on a stone. Another leap and he's at the base of the lighthouse. Without hesitation, he begins to scramble up the wall, his limbs stretched wide, his tiny toes and fingers finding the smallest cracks and seams, chips of paint, rough texture in the siding.

"What the hell?" I ask, glancing at the others. Xela and Uzula are grinning in appreciation at Kale's skill.

"Maybe I'm the one who should be jealous," Harmon mutters, sliding a possessive arm around me.

"Not funny," I say, giving him a playful punch. But my attention is quickly drawn back to Kale, who has reached the window. He slips through and disappears. A minute later, he reappears in the window, climbs onto the ledge, and leaps. I have to hold back a scream as he plummets fifty feet towards the ground. But somehow, he lands on his feet, catlike, halfway across the jumble of vines.

Straightening, he shakes his head.

"She's not there?" I ask. "Yvonne told Astrid to bring her here."

"Figures," Xela mutters. "I never trusted her."

"You think?" I say. "She took my shifting."

"If she's not here," Harmon says. "There's only one way to find her. It's time to talk to your mother."

Without another word, he turns and starts down the mountain. The rest of us fall in behind. "You're sure she's not up there but…dead?" Uzula whispers, her black hair gleaming in the sunlight, each strand nearly prismatic with shimmer.

"I'm sure," Kale says, his lip trembling.

I try to steel myself for the worst. If my mother was bad, I can only imagine what Yvonne is capable of.

26

As we make our way into the wolf valley, my muscles begin to clench, drawing tight to my bones. I've barely had my body back for an hour, and we're going to confront my attacker already? I don't know if I'm ready. I need time to think. Catching up with Harmon, I grab his arm.

"Don't we need a plan or something?" I ask. "We can't just charge in, guns blazing."

"No guns," he says, holding up both hands. But behind his smile, his eyes are fierce and determined.

"Yeah, but…"

"But nothing," he says. "She tried to kill my mate. She took your friend. She tried to take my pack from me, and she's not even a wolf."

"So you're just going to find her and kill her?"

"No," he says. "I'm going to challenge her."

"What if…?" I can't finish the thought. It's too terrible.

"What if I lose?" His jaw is set, and his eyes bore into mine. "That's not going to happen."

"Can I just borrow Stella a second?" Xela asks, slipping her hand into the crook of my elbow. She motions for Harmon to keep on, and after his eyes catch with mine a moment, he turns and continues down the mountain.

"What are you doing?" Xela hisses. "Don't show him

you're afraid he might lose. He needs confidence. You're supposed to believe in him."

"Yeah, but what if he does lose?" I whisper back.

"You're a shifter," she says. "You don't mate for life."

But I know she's wrong. Whether it's my werewolf mother's genes or just something in me, I know I'll never love anyone the way I love Harmon. Rabidly, painfully, eternally.

When we reach the valley floor, Harmon stops at the stream that runs behind his old house. I'm surprised to see that they've left it standing, a blackened shell of the community center it once was. Only the front porch and front wall are still in good condition. I take Harmon's hand and squeeze, smiling up at him. "I'm sorry if I sounded doubtful," I say. "You're going to win."

He cocks an eyebrow and smiles down at me. "What do I get if I win?"

"You get me," I say, sliding my free arm around his neck and pressing my body to his. "And you better win, because I don't mate with losers." I stand on tiptoes and kiss him. When I pull away, he's looking at me with hungry, determined eyes.

I shiver for the fate of that evil woman.

"You won't," he says, his jaw tightening. "If I don't win, it's because I'm dead. There's no loser."

I swallow hard. "It's a fight to the death?"

"Yes, or the other wolf can choose permanent exile from the Three Valleys. The Winslow witches put a protection on the valleys centuries ago. Anyone exiled can never set foot in the valleys again. But I'm not going in thinking of exile. I'm going in for the kill."

I nod, my breath catching. I have to remind myself this is how wolves are. He's not being brutal, he's being a good Alpha and a good mate, protecting us. Who knows what her sorcery can do, what tricks she could play to get through the witches' shield.

Harmon pulls me in and kisses me hard. "Let's go."

Our little band marches through the community, along the path to Mother's house. But instead of turning down the sloping drive, Harmon squares his shoulders and continues on.

"Where are we going?" I ask.

"I summoned the pack," Harmon says darkly.

When we step into the clearing where they hold their lunar meetings, where they shift into wolves once a month, where they celebrated what was supposed to be Harmon's coronation, I see what he means. Almost everyone is here, but as I look around, it looks like a sparser group than the last time I was here. I scan for my sisters, for my mother's body, but they are not here.

"Where are the others?" I whisper.

"The ones who are loyal to your mother do not answer my call," he says. "I don't have a pack bond with her or her followers." I can tell by the haughty tone of his voice that he's hiding the wound that causes his pride.

The wolves stir, and a murmur goes through the pack when Harmon appears with us. I meet their curious gazes without dropping my eyes. Since we took them in, they haven't been hostile to me. But they also probably knew I was supposedly dead, and that Harmon kept my body in his house, waiting for me to wake up.

"What's going on here?" a voice demands behind us.

It's a voice that now sends a chill down my spine, now that I recognize the cadence that is not my mother's. I should have guessed sooner.

Her eyes rake over me, and for a moment, I see a depth of fury I didn't know was possible. It hits me like a banshee's scream, racing along my skin, down my spine. But she recovers herself quickly, composes her face into an approximation of a smile.

Harmon turns to face her. "I'm glad you answered my summons."

"Don't flatter yourself," she says. "I just came to see what you were trying to pull this time."

Harmon squares his shoulders. "As rightful leader of this pack, I challenge you for the position of Alpha."

A collective inhalation from the pack meets this declaration. I glance at the others, but no one meets my eyes.

"It's about time," Yvonne drawls in an artificially light tone.

"Since a fight for the pack requires all members in attendance, you'll have to go and gather your followers," Harmon says coldly. "Since you cannot communicate through the pack bond."

Yvonne stands there a few seconds, looking furious, then turns and storms off.

"I thought you couldn't communicate with them, either," I whisper.

"These members pledged loyalty to me," he says quietly. "While you were sleeping. I'm their Alpha already."

I try not to think about Harmon gnawing on all these people and drinking their blood.

After a minute, Yvonne returns, her head held high. "My minions are fetching the others," she says. "Now let's get started. How does this work?"

I notice some of the others frowning, and decide that's probably something she should already know.

"I will fight to the death for my pack and what I think is best for them," Harmon says. "My leadership will be fair to all, and I will bring unity with the other valleys in a way that benefits this pack."

Yvonne laughs, that high-pitched laugh I should have known could never come from my mother. Now that I see Yvonne in her body, it's hard to believe I was so blind I couldn't see it before. My mother would never coordinate a fall palette for her outfit the way Yvonne has—camel colored ankle boots with patterned boot socks scrunched down above them, skinny black jeans, a cream cashmere sweater, and a rust-colored scarf.

"I've brought unity with the shifters," Yvonne says. "I've allied myself with their new queen, as well as some of the witches. I'm obviously the better diplomat. And you're barely more than a baby. Do you even shave yet?" Her lip curls in a sneer, but Harmon's face remains steady and fierce.

Voices on the trail distract me, and the next moment, the rest of the pack arrives, led by a breathless Zora. She's dressed better, too, though not as noticeably in her ripped jeans, lace-up ankle boots, and olive-green sweater with a plaid scarf. Still, there is something disheveled about the whole pack, as if they can't maintain order without an Alpha. They bump into each other when taking position behind Yvonne. Their numbers are less than when they camped with us, which must be a result of Yvonne pushing for an alliance with the shifters. I'm surprised to see that in her pack are not only the remaining wolves, but a few strangers.

"Witches," Zora whispers. I startle, not having noticed her slipping in beside me.

I survey Yvonne's bunch and spot Astrid in a tight circle with some more strangers, who must be her shifters. "What is she doing here?" I hiss, nodding in her direction.

"Mother's weirdly obsessed with her," Elidi says, joining us. "She practically lives with us. Mother says she's teaching her to be a queen." Our eyes catch, and that unspoken connection between us tugs at me. All that time, I just wanted to be her sister. I wanted a family so badly that when it was offered by an imposter, I jumped at the chance, too blinded by that fantasy to see that it wasn't my mother doing the offering at all.

"Fat lot of good it's done," Zora says. "She's not even a wolf. I don't know why she's here."

It strikes me then, as I look at Astrid's pinched, determined face, that she's in the exact position I was in when I came here. The object of Zora's scorn, a trespasser in the valley, at the mercy of her mother. A pang of sympathy goes out to her before I remember that I hate her.

"I challenge you for leadership of this pack," Harmon says, his voice rising over the others, commanding their silence. It strikes me how different he is than the night of the eclipse. He was a boy then. He's a man now, ready for this role. Pride swells within me.

He's *my* man. *My* Alpha.

"I accept," Yvonne says, her lip curling.

"I will fight as a wolf," Harmon says.

Yvonne is silent. A few of her supporters shift and exchange glances.

A twitch below Harmon's eye betrays his fury at this imposter trying to steal his pack, but the rest of his face remains blank. "Will you fight me as a wolf or a human?" he prompts.

"A human," she says decisively, and it strikes me that she may not be able to shift. She's not a werewolf. I'm not sure if that magic lies in the body or the spirit, but I'm guessing by her answer that she can't do it.

A few of her supporters mutter in protest. She smiles slyly. "You're going to rip apart a woman twice your age with your teeth? What a brave leader you are."

I open my mouth, my heart pounding, ready to warn Harmon. She's going to pull some dirty trick, I can feel it. I should have warned him earlier. She always has something up her sleeve. But Elidi catches my wrist and silences me with a look. "You have to trust him," she says. "He knows what he's doing."

I swallow my resentment. She doesn't know who he's really up against. But I hold my tongue and force myself to watch.

"You understand the terms of this match," says the pack's elder, an ancient-looking woman who I saw on my very first day here. "You may fight to the death or ask for the mercy rule and choose permanent exile from the Three Valleys, effective immediately. You may not go home first or collect your things. You must leave from the fight, in whatever condition you are in. You are thereby dead to us. No one in attendance may assist you if you choose this path. The Alpha who remains is our true Alpha and will retain the loyalty of every member of the pack."

"I understand," Harmon says, his fists clenching and unclenching, his body almost vibrating with that uncontainable energy of his. He wants this. He's waited so long, trying to be diplomatic, accepting my mother because she is a pack member. But now that he knows she's not my mother, he can't wait to destroy her.

"I understand," Yvonne echoes.

"May our true Alpha win," the elder says, stepping back to join the others. "Commence fighting."

Harmon instantly rips off his shirt and drops his shorts.

"Oooh, goodie," Xela says, gripping my hand. As Elidi grips my other arm, I can feel her shaking.

Yvonne charges forward, her shoulder ramming Harmon's middle. She grabs his arm and yanks him off his feet, flipping him over her back.

"He hasn't had time to transition," I whisper, panic rippling through me.

Instead of fighting back, he's trying to shift into wolf form as quickly as possible. In these moments, he's completely vulnerable. Yvonne hurls him to the ground, leaps on him, and grabs him in a headlock, twisting his head back so forcefully we can all hear bones snapping.

A howl rips from his throat, and his jaws snap. Wolf jaws, I see with relief. For a strange moment, he's that beast I fell in love with, half-human, half-wolf. Fur races along his bare legs, which are shorter than they were seconds ago, slimmer. His mouth is a wolf's mouth, his human hair still thick on his rounded cranium.

Yvonne squeezes her arms around his neck from behind and gouges at his eyes. His claws scrabble against her, shredding her sweater. With a last heave, his wolf emerges, and I let out a breath. My whole body is trembling, adrenaline coursing through me. If I need to jump in and defend him, I will, I don't care what the wolf code of conduct says. He's my mate, and I'll die, too, before I let that bitch kill him.

If she expected him to take it easy on her because she chose to fight as a human, she's dead wrong. He squirms from her grasp and drops to the ground, then instantly spins and sinks his teeth into her thigh. She screams in pain and slams her fist into his skull. He jumps back, and my heart staggers at the dazed look in his eyes. She must have called on more than her ordinary human strength. Otherwise, she's defenseless.

By choice, I remind myself.

Still, I flinch when he lunges at her and tears into her leg. Fabric comes away with flesh, and I squeeze my eyes closed. Elidi's nails bite painfully into my arm. "Open your eyes," she growls. "What will he think if he looks over and sees you won't even watch him fight for you? He'll think you think he's a monster for killing your mother. Do you think that?"

"No," I say, forcing my eyes open. I'm just in time to see him knock Yvonne to the ground and go for her throat. But before he gets there, he stops short, as if pulling taut against an invisible leash. He lets out a howl of pain and fury.

"She's doing something to him," I whisper, grabbing Elidi's arm. "That's not our mother. It's a mirror."

Her eyes widen. "What?"

"Harmon didn't want to say anything, because she'd say he was making up stories, that it showed how crazy he was, or that he was afraid to fight her. We have no proof. But I know it. She told me, when she put me in that tree."

Elidi looks doubtfully at me and then the fight, biting her lip.

A flash of horror goes through me when Harmon whines and backs off Yvonne, throwing his head back as if to howl. No sound comes out his muzzle. Is she trying to take over his body? What if she does? In a wolf's body, she could kill anyone here. I've put every member of the pack in terrible danger.

Harmon shakes his head and dives forward, snapping at Yvonne. But something is wrong. His eyes look unfocused, blind. She kicks at him, hitting him square in the chest.

"She has been different," Elidi admits. "But if it's not her..."

"Can I step in if she's not really a wolf? It's not a fair fight."

"No," she says, her lips tightening. "He wouldn't want you to. He knew, right? And still he chose a fight to the death. If you stepped in, you'd humiliate and emasculate him. You'd make him look weak in front of the pack. He'd never live it down."

Just then, Harmon lets out a roar of fury and leaps on Yvonne, knocking her to the ground again. In a blur of movement, he lunges for her throat and sinks his teeth into her jugular.

I almost collapse, biting back the hysterical giggle of

relief and victory threatening to bubble forth. He's got her. I'm not the only one fighting the urge to cheer out loud. The crowd is mesmerized, their excited, wide eyes fixed on their leader. Elidi is holding her breath, biting her lip. A little girl shifts into wolf form in her father's arms and yips until her mother shushes her.

"It's not over," I remind Elidi, but I'm really telling myself, bringing myself back to the very real danger that remains. "She could take over his body, rip out his soul."

Elidi shudders, but her eyes are sparkling with exhilaration and pride as she watches Harmon pin the struggling sorceress. "This is pack life," she says, her eyes riveted on the fight. "He's proving himself as Alpha to the whole pack. Whoever wins this will gain the loyalty of all of us."

She breaks off, her eyes widening. A flash of light catches my eye, and I turn to see Yvonne's fist raised high behind Harmon's head, a knife glinting in her hand. Even as Harmon's teeth stay clamped on her throat, and blood soaks the ground around them, she can't resist one more dirty trick. She plunges the knife into Harmon's back.

27

A scream rips from my throat. I try to break free of the pack, but my sisters and Fernando wrestle me back.

"What part of *to-the-death* do you not understand?" Zora says. "This is not your fight, Stella. You don't see me running out there to rescue my mom."

"Don't look away," Elidi says, jerking on my arm so hard I have to look. "He's still alive. Stop distracting him or he might lose grip."

She's right. His teeth are still clamped on Yvonne's neck, crushing it even as the knife hilt sticks up from his back. I want to run to him, hold him and help him. Instead, I force myself to watch, to send him silent cheers, prayers, and love. At last, her body goes limp all at once, and Harmon struggles to his feet.

Elidi releases me, and a distracted part of me realizes that she must have been rooting for Harmon. But I can't dwell on that now. Something is pulling at me, a familiar and terrifying. Panic rips through me, and I gasp, clutching at my heart. But it's not something I can stop with my human strength. For once, it's not my frail human body's job to fight the intruder.

It's up to me. The part of me that has nothing to do with whether I'm a human or a tiger or a freaking tree. I can feel Yvonne's invading force, can feel her trying to rip me free again. It's the same repulsive feeling as before. My tiger roars in fury, claws to get out. But she couldn't help me now even if she was free.

Yvonne's furious, desperate energy claws into my throat, choking off my air. I sink down on one knee, fighting for breath. Images of my worst moments through my mind—when I found my father's body, the funeral, the loneliness and despair of Mother's attic, my sisters' betrayal, my father's callous attitude towards me. No one loves me. I see Harmon dancing with another girl at his coronation, his hands on her waist, his eyes locked on hers. The hateful, accusatory glare when I hurt his father.

The guilt of the fire crashes through me. No one should love me. I left Elidi when she wanted to escape the valley with me. I left my father when he risked his life to come back for me. I left Harmon in the basement alone, refused to be his mate even when he'd Chosen me for life. It's my fault that the wolves lost a huge part of their hunting grounds. It's my fault Haven is missing. It's my fault my father is really dead, and this time, he's not coming back.

I don't have to continue this life where everyone loathes me, and with good reason. I could let go. Give someone a chance to do what's right, to do the things I couldn't do. I could fly up and out, the way I did when Astrid told me to run.

It's Harmon's voice that cuts through the chaos of my despair. "Don't listen to her."

My head jerks up, and I catch sight of Astrid across the

clearing. Her lips are moving so fast they're a blur, her eyes unfocused. She's doing a spell. I can only hope it's not directed at me, because I can't fight her off, too. I remember my mother's words.

Maybe it was because I'd left my body before, and the bond that held me to it was never the same.

I can feel her twisting my soul, forcing her way in. I can't stop her. Mother was right. She'll never stop until I'm dead.

But I am stronger than my mother. I am stronger than any wolf. Stronger than Astrid. Stronger than Yvonne. And this is my body, not hers.

It's only a frail human body, one I once scorned. But it's mine. And I am more than my body. I'm a vulnerable human girl, but I'm also a fucking tiger.

I'm done with people telling me what I can and can't be. Tired of people telling me what I am, controlling me, using me. This is my life. My body. My choice.

With a roar of fury, I thrust myself fully into my solid, meaty human body. I feel a pulse of fury, anguish, and pain. And then she's gone. Unsteadily, I push myself to my feet and look around. No one seems to notice what just happened. They are crowded around Harmon.

Except Astrid. A tiny, tentative smile twitches at the corner of her mouth like a question. But I don't have time for her now. I shove through the crowd, drop to my knees, and throw my arms around Harmon. Kissing his bloody fur, I hold his face between my hands. He's still a wolf. And yet…I know I heard him speak.

"You're going to be okay," I tell him. "If it was a mortal wound, you'd be dead."

But I don't entirely believe my own words. Harmon is unsteady on his feet, his eyes glazed with pain. He lowers his head, and a spasm runs through his body like a last, shuddering breath. I almost cry out. But when another comes, and another, I realize he is shifting back to human.

"Wait," I cry. "Are you sure that's safe? What if the knife is positioned differently, against a vital organ?"

The crowd shifts, and the familiar figure of Dr. Golden steps through, braids swinging. "Let me have a look," she says in her soft, no-nonsense voice. She gently lays Harmon on his side and presses her fingertips to his throat. The crowd shifts closer, murmuring with concern. What if both their Alphas die in the battle? No one explained what happened then.

"Damn cheat," someone curses. "I knew she'd pull something."

So they weren't supposed to have weapons. It makes sense, but I also wonder why anyone would choose to stay human to fight.

"I'm going to pull the blade out," Dr. Golden says, handing me a clean hand towel. "Press this to the wound to stop the bleeding."

I do as she instructs. I expect Harmon to be carried away on a stretcher, but as soon as the knife is out, he starts trying to shift again. For a minute, I don't think he'll be able to. But after three times the length of time it normally takes, he transitions to human. His body is tall and brown, more muscular than I remembered after the spring he's spent rebuilding houses.

He looks every inch an Alpha.

Taking the cloth from my hand, he holds it pressed to

the back of his neck. "I am your Alpha," he barks at the crowd. "But if you don't accept that, I won't make you swear loyalty. If you remain loyal to that imposter, exile yourself."

He glowers at the pack standing to Yvonne's side of the clearing. They all look nervous, guilty, and solemn.

"I won't have a pack with divided loyalty," Harmon continues. "And I won't force you to swear an oath you don't mean. If anyone does not wish to be a member of this pack, under my leadership, leave now." Despite the slight tremor in his body, his eyes are blazing with white-hot fury.

A few of Mother's supporters take a knee, but Harmon glares at them. "I am not a king," he says. "Get up off your knees. No one needs to grovel. Whatever you've done, if you're in this pack, it's forgiven. This pack is one being, each member his own wolf and part of the larger wolf that is the pack itself."

The two men who knelt jump to their feet, looking chagrined.

"But if you ever question my authority again," Harmon growls. "You won't have the honor of kneeling."

The men nod quickly, their Adam's apples bobbing in unison.

Harmon draws a slow, ragged breath, quiet enough that the others can't hear. I slip under his arm, and he nearly collapses onto me. The towel on his neck is soaked through with blood.

"This is my mate," he growls. "I have Chosen her. If anyone objects to this alliance, you may leave this pack and find one elsewhere. I intend to make peace in the

Three Valleys with her at my side, and one day, whether we have pups or cubs, they will be accepted into this pack if they so choose. Are we all in agreement?"

A cheer goes up.

"Do I have your support?" Harmon calls. "Do I have your loyalty?"

The pack cheers louder, a cry echoing through the valley and up the mountainsides around us. Somewhere, I think I hear a whisper of the ghosts cheering, too.

While the crowd is still loud, Harmon turns his face and speaks into my ear. "Get me out of here before I pass out. My first act as their Alpha can't be to collapse."

"Done," I say, tightening my arm around his waist. I hold up a hand to the crowd, then raise my own voice. "Your Alpha has fought bravely, but he needs medical assistance. And I need to administer the kind of care only a mate can. So please don't hold it against me if I steal him away for a few minutes."

Some people actually laugh, and most look only vaguely uncomfortable in my presence instead of horrified, as they did when I arrived in the valley. Maybe now they know that I am not a body-snatcher, that I can control myself. But as we make our way through the crowd, Harmon leaning on me more heavily than either of us let on, my mind circles back to that moment Yvonne stopped fighting for control of my body.

If she abandoned my mother's body voluntarily, she could have entered someone else's body when I wouldn't give up my own? My eyes search the crowd for a sign of her devious, malicious eyes.

When Harmon stumbles, I am pulled back to the

most important task. I have a mate to take care of. Yvonne
will never keep me from him again.

28

An hour later, while Dr. Golden attends to Harmon, I slip out and return to Mother's house. I wish her house had burned along with Harmon's. Setting foot inside it floods me with too many dark and depressing memories. But I have to see Astrid.

When I get there, though, my sisters say she disappeared over the mountain with the other shifters after the fight. But when I tell them I need to ask her about Haven, they cast strange glances at each other.

"What?" I ask. "You know where she is?"

"She's in your room," Elidi says, looking at the floor.

I race up the stairs, not waiting for an explanation. Haven is lying on the floor, on her back, and for a second, I almost choke on my breath. But she sits up and turns, and relief floods through me. "I thought you were dead," I cry, racing to her side. She's chained to the chimney, the same way I was. "What happened?" I ask, dropping to my knees and throwing my arms around her.

"And here I thought my love would always be unrequited," she says, hugging me back.

I pull away, laughing and trying not to cry at the same time. "Your collective doesn't know where you are," I say. "They're beside themselves. They never heard anything about you. They had no idea where you'd gone."

"They better not have joined another witch's collective," she growls, scooping her fox into her arms. It sits on its hind legs in her lap, staring at me with bright, shiny eyes.

"At least she let you have your fox," I say, slumping against the end of the couch that, for so long, was my bed.

"The only reason she let me have him is because she wanted to force me to use my magic, and she knew I wouldn't be able to do much without my familiar."

"Why didn't you tell me she was your aunt?"

Haven laughs and strokes her fox's head. "I thought you'd be weirded out that I'm related to a sorceress. She lived next door when I was a kid, and she taught me to protect her during her projections."

"Good thing, too," I mutter.

"She made me call her *Auntie*. Gag." Haven shudders dramatically.

As much as I love Haven, it's a relief that she's not yet another one of my sisters. I keep waiting for more to pop up at any moment. "Actually, she lived next door to me, too," I tell Haven. "But she was in an old lady body at the time."

"I can imagine how much she hated that," Haven says. "She was always trying out new potions to make herself younger and prettier. She used to have me come over and check on whatever body she's dragged home to make sure it was still alive when she projected into something else. Talk about childhood trauma."

"I wish you'd told me."

"I didn't want you to think all witches were like that," she says with a shrug.

"Wait, are you saying you care what someone thinks of you?"

"No," she says with a scowl. "And anyway, it wouldn't have made any difference. I didn't know she'd possessed your mother. I might not have even known if I'd met your mother."

"You're right," I say. "I didn't tell you I knew her, either, and for pretty much the same reason."

"Cool. Now that we're all good with each other, you think you could get me out of this chain?"

"Oh, I'm so sorry!" I say, jumping to my feet. "Let me ask my sisters for the key. I'll be right back."

"You better," she calls as I rush down the stairs. After seeing Mother chain me up for years, it must not have seemed strange for my sisters to see her do it to someone she claimed had tried to kill her daughter. When they give me the key, I race back up to let Haven go. She promises to visit, but wastes no time in returning to her collective and the hive.

When she's gone, I accept Elidi's shy invitation to stay for a dinner of overcooked vegetables and unidentified meat. While we eat, my sisters fill me in on how Haven ended up there. When Dr. Golden declared that someone had given me some kind of sleep potion, Yvonne suddenly and miraculously recovered a memory of Haven casting a spell on me. The wolves returned to their valley, but Yvonne snuck up and somehow retrieved Haven from the tower. No one knew she was there except my sisters, who were sworn to secrecy, and her precious Astrid.

"I should have known it wasn't Mother," Zora says,

sloshing her spoon back and forth in her bowl. "She'd never bring a witch into our house."

"You couldn't have known," Elidi says, patting Zora's hand.

"I'm going to lie down," Zora says, pushing back from the table. "I don't feel so good."

"You need me to sleep in your room with you tonight?" Elidi asks, her eyes full of concern.

"Your cooking is probably why I feel sick," Zora says, stomping out of the room and up the stairs.

Elidi casts me an apologetic look. I feel like an intruder who witnessed a private moment between sisters. I get the feeling this isn't the first time Elidi stayed in Zora's room to make her feel safe. After all, they have been living with a crazy sorceress for months. They share a bond I'll never be a part of, no matter how many dinner invitations I accept. They have been sisters all their lives.

My chest tightens, and suddenly I'm not hungry, either. "I better go check on Harmon," I say, pushing back from the table. "I want to be there when he wakes up."

Before I go, I retrieve the padlock from the chain upstairs and throw it down the outhouse.

29

For the next week, Harmon recovers in his new place. I hate that he lost his big Alpha house, but at the same time, I don't really want to live in any house where I was held captive—even one with good memories as well as bad. I hang around Harmon's bedside until I get on his nerves by asking if he's okay every ten minutes. Finally, when he's fully recovered except for a bandage on the back of his neck, I ask if I can go out.

"You don't have to ask permission," he says, looking at me strangely.

"Right," I say, forcing a laugh. "I guess I'm still not used to living among wolves. When I lived here before, I would never have just gone out and walked around the community."

"I'm sorry about that, Stella," he says. "I should have done something about her a long time ago."

"That day," I begin, sinking onto the foot of his bed. "When you fought her. What did she do to you?"

"She made me see things I didn't want to see," he says slowly. "It was like having a blindfold over my eyes, with the worst things I could imagine pictured on it. I couldn't close my eyes to it. But luckily, my other senses worked just fine."

I take his hand and squeeze. I can imagine what she

made him see—she put those thoughts in my head, too. Still, I feel silly saying the next words. "When she left my mother's body…I heard you speak."

Harmon shrugs. "We have a bond, too. You may not be a wolf, but you're my mate."

"When she stopped…do you think she died? What if she entered someone else's body and we don't know?"

"I don't want any distrust within the pack," he says. "But I'll keep an eye on them if you're worried about it. I don't want you to be afraid."

"I want us all to be safe, that's all. I want her gone."

Harmon squeezes my hand, his face serious. "I'm sure after what happened with your mom, it will be hard for you to trust people. And I don't just mean Yvonne."

"It's over now," I say. "It doesn't matter. I'm not mad at Talia anymore."

"That's big of you," he says, pulling me to him. "That's the kind of thing that makes me know I Chose the right person. Despite everything that's happened to you, you're still good." He pulls me down on his lap and draws me in for a kiss.

"I don't know about that," I murmur against his lips. "Sometimes I can be as bad as all you big bad wolves."

His teeth graze my lip. "Is that right?"

"Mmmhmmm." I nip at his lip in return.

He pulls back, and his blue eyes lock on mine. "I love you, Stella. The good side, the bad side, every side of you fascinates and captivates me. And I know I'll keep finding more sides to you all my life, and they'll still catch me by surprise. I'm always going to want to know more about you. I'm always going to want to be the person you tell your stories to, the person you cry to, the person you run to when you need protection. Let me protect you. Let me comfort you. Let me listen to you."

"Okay," I whisper.

"Let me make you my mate," he says. "Officially. There's an eclipse in a couple months. We're going to do a coronation of sorts. Everyone is eager to retake their oath of loyalty. I think I can wait that long."

I swallow hard. "For...?"

"For you," he says, winding a strand of my frizzled hair behind my ear. No matter how much I comb it, I can't undo the damage of the heat that day and leaving it unkempt for so long.

"You have me," I say.

"For us to be officially mated," he says. "To have the mating ceremony."

"We don't actually have to, you know, *mate* in front of people, right?"

Harmon laughs. "No, kitten. It's like a wedding."

"We're so young," I point out.

"I know you're the only one," he says. "I'm sure. I've Chosen. It can't be undone. My bond with you won't change when I'm twenty, or a hundred and twenty. I have no reason to wait. But if you do, I'll wait. Like I said, mine never changes. So for me, it doesn't matter when we have the ceremony. You're the mystery."

I hesitate. I've been hesitating for four years. I've been timid, meek. I've let other people make my decisions. I've let people decide what I can be, who I can be, what freedoms I deserve. This time, I want to make my own decision. I want to do something wild, like the animal I am.

Something bold, worthy of my tiger. I'm tired of being weak. I'm ready to do what I want. And I'm finally free to do it.

A slow smile spreads across my face. "No," I say. "I'm done waiting. I'm ready to live. So...yes."

"You'll be my mate?"

"I'm already your mate," I say. "I always have been. You just didn't know it."

He quirks an eyebrow. "And you did?"

"I might have," I tease, remembering the jolt I felt the first time we met. "But I guess you'll never know. Since I'm such a mystery and all."

Harmon laughs, and when I join him, it's the most beautiful sound I've ever heard.

30

The next weeks pass in a blur. I take walks around the community, letting people see me, get used to me. I call out a greeting to everyone I see, and most of them answer.

A few weeks later, the wolves go out hunting on the full moon, and for the first time since returning to the valley, I feel alone. Lonely.

But just when I'm ready to start feeling sorry for myself, a knock comes at the door. I rush to open it, hoping Harmon has come back from hunting early. Instead, a troop of misfits marches in, dropping dirt and leaves on the floor as they go. A red fox darts in with them and begins sniffing around the legs of all the furniture.

"You're domesticated," Haven says, giving me a sly smile.

I feel my face warm as they examine my new house. Harmon assures me it's our "starter house," that we'll fill a big lodge full of children one day. But I'm happy with my tiny log cabin.

"Not bad," Yorn grumbles, hooking his stubby thumbs into the straps of his overalls and rocking back on his heels.

"What? Did Yorn pay me a compliment?" I ask.

"I think he did," Xela crows.

"I said the house looked okay, not you," Yorn says.

We all burst out laughing, and something twists in my chest. At first, it's so foreign I almost don't recognize it. I think it's a pain from missing them. But then I realize it's a fullness so complete I feel like I'll explode. I may never have the family I yearned for all those years—a conventional family. But I have this family.

I have my wolf family, too, which is warming up to me.

I have my shifter family, which I haven't even begun to explore.

And I have Harmon. In just a few months, we'll be mated. Someday, we might get married, but for now, we're doing the wolf version. One day, we'll have a family of our own. No, it's not what I pictured all those years, when I wanted to be my mother's daughter, beloved as my sisters, or my father's daughter. But all these people have adopted me, in their way. I belong.

31

Finally, Coronation Day arrives. I can't help but linger on thoughts of the one that was disrupted almost two years ago. My life is so completely different, I couldn't have imagined it, let alone believed it, if someone had told me then. And I'm not the only one who is different. The community is different.

Harmon is a warmer leader than his father, more compassionate. After he'd recovered, Harmon swallowed his pride and asked the witches forgiveness for the wrongful accusations the wolves had cast on Haven. In turn, the witches apologized for Yvonne, who had caused so much mischief.

The mountainside is still blackened from the fire, but the witches allow the wolves to come and go, hunting in the First Valley. In return, the witches come to dig roots and collect herbs in our valley and get water from our springs. The lines between the territories aren't gone, but they are beginning to blur. Some witches even come to visit and bring medicines and tinctures, and the wolves' suspicion is thawing. And, of course, my motley crew of rogues visits every few weeks.

The only thing that hasn't changed much is our relationship with the shifters. Although they no longer attack, they do not mingle with the wolves. Harmon often ponders ways to reach out to them, but I'm too angry at Astrid for her evildoing to offer much help. At least I know my tiger is still alive inside me, even if I can't let her out. One day, when we do the witches a favor, Harmon says he'll ask for help reversing the spell. But we don't want to ask for too much, too fast.

On the morning of the eclipse day, I'm just beginning to comb out my hair when footsteps cross the floor of our living room.

"You can't see me in my dress," I tease. I've told Harmon I want a real wedding one day, with all the traditions. But not yet. Tonight, there will be no rings, no legal documents. This is a bond inside us.

But I still want the fun of surprising him.

"It's us," Elidi says, sticking her head around the door of the bedroom. "Can we come in?"

"We need help with our makeup," Zora says, pushing open the door and marching in. She's carrying a large, flat box in front of her like a shield.

"Yeah, see, you can't order me around anymore," I remind her. "In fact...I guess since I'm marrying the Alpha, I'll be able to order you around."

"Ha," she says. "Don't count on it."

I laugh. "I won't."

"Give it to her," Elidi says, nodding at me.

Zora sighs. "Fine, we brought you a present. It's not wrapped. And you have to open it now."

She thrusts the heavy cardboard box at me. I peel the tape off the end and tip it onto the bed. The heavy mirror slides out, and for a moment, my breath catches. I remember polishing the ornate curls of wood around the edges until they gleamed, and how betrayed I felt when Mother let her take it. I remember hauling it up and down the stairs when I cared for Zora when she was injured, how it felt like she was rubbing it in my face that she had the mirror and I couldn't do a thing about it. I remember how many times I considered "accidentally" dropping it so I didn't have to endure her smugness. I remember seeing my father in it.

"Thank you," I say, standing and throwing my arms around her.

She stiffens and pats my back. "Now can you help with our makeup?"

I laugh and set the mirror on the dresser. "Sure. And thank you. I mean it."

"Whatever," she says. "Don't spy on me."

"I hope I don't have to," I say, turning to Elidi. "You know you can come visit any time you want. Not just when you need a favor. I'm just down the path."

For the rest of the day, Elidi casts odd glances at me, and that only makes the sense of déjà vous more intense. For all the years I was at Mother's, Elidi gave me those looks. Looks that said she wanted to talk to me, but couldn't. But when I ask her what's going on, she just looks away and says she's nervous. I wonder if she's afraid the shifters will attack again, as I am.

By evening, we're all dressed up and ready to go. The group from the mountain has joined us, though they'll have to leave before the pack transitions, which is a sacred time that is supposed to be witnessed only by wolves. Even I don't stay past dinner at the monthly lunar meetings. I tell Harmon that's my time to spend with the rogues, which is partly true. But I also do it out of respect for the pack. I don't want them to have to ask me to leave, don't want them to have to wonder if it's acceptable. There are things we don't share, and I'm happy with that.

Tonight, Haven is in one of her crazy outfits, her hair filled with feathers and fall leaves, her dress an odd assortment of fabrics and textures all patched together, and her fox serving as a scarf. Xela wears a dress, too, but with her leggings, she manages to look as much like Robin Hood as ever. Uzula wears a tunic that is made entirely of fur, and Kale stands stiffly inside a powder blue leisure suit.

"They don't share the same fashion sense as humans, do they?" Zora whispers to me when they're busy fixing Yorn's twisted suspenders.

Zora wears a backless royal blue gown with a slit up the thigh, sexy as ever. Elidi wears a simple, pale pink cotton dress, as far from the frills and tulle of the last eclipse as possible.

"I told her to get something nicer," Zora whispers to me when Elidi's back is turned. "It's like she's trying not to be pretty."

I watch Elidi looking at herself in the mirror, and a pang of sadness goes through me. I've been so busy trying to adjust to one crazy circumstance and then the next, that I almost forgot that she once wanted to get out of here as much as I did. When I found out I was a shifter, I decided that life outside these valleys was over for me. Instead of wanting to escape, I wanted to find out more—about my family, my abilities, myself.

I never imagined I'd end up here, as the Alpha's mate. There is still so much for me to learn, though, so much to find out. And I'm happy I'll be doing it with Harmon by my side. But as happy as I am now, Elidi's circumstances haven't changed. She's never found her mate. She's never gotten away. More than anyone, I know that's the reason she's not putting in any effort.

"You'll find your mate one day, too," I say, slipping up beside her at the mirror. Her white hair is still smooth, unlike mine, which is wooly and damaged. Tonight, though, mine is pulled back in an up do, while Elidi's hangs long around her shoulders.

"I know," she says, smiling serenely at her reflection.

For the first time, I wonder if she's found someone, and I can't help feeling betrayed that she didn't tell me. I remind myself that we aren't close, that I need to work harder to be a part of their lives, too.

32

As we take the dirt path towards the community gathering place, I glance around at the trees, now awash in amber, gold, red, yellow, and rust. I send them a silent greeting, as I always do. A chill has crept into the air, and once again, I remember the last time I walked this path towards a coronation. At first I was trying to escape with Mrs. Nguyen, before I knew what she really was. And later, I walked this path in Elidi's shoes, pretending to be her.

Laughter wells inside me at the memory, and a warmth sweeps through me when I realize I can tell them the story. I'm not alone anymore. And so, as we walk to the clearing, I recount my nerves the last time I did this, how I couldn't find Elidi's sweater, how I was sure someone would spot my imitation. They laugh with me, Zora and Haven and Xela howling with it, apparently becoming fast friends, and Elidi chuckling quietly with Kale and Uzula. As ever, Yorn stomps along frowning.

The moment we step into the clearing, Harmon's head swivels towards us. Our eyes meet, his pale blue eyes capturing mine and refusing to let go. My heart leaps in my chest, and my feet tangle with each other. I bump against Haven, who slips an arm around my waist and squeezes. "Hey, I know that's your man, but if these patriarchal weres ever start getting too much for your shifter soul, there's always a spot in my collective for you."

"Thanks," I say, laughing. "But I think I'm good. The only thing I'm missing is my tiger. So if you ever figure out how to undo that spell…"

It's true, too. Everything in my life is perfect—except my trapped tigress. There will always be a part of me that's incomplete without her. But patience is a skill I've mastered well.

Even an angry tiger cannot keep me from enjoying this night, though. Like last time, my heart hammers as I make my way across the clearing. But this time, I float in my gauzy white dress. My feet are bare, my toes sinking into the cool grass as twilight falls around us. The insects of summer still sing, though quieter now, and the hum of voices dies down when I approach Harmon.

"You look like an angel," he says. "White hair, white dress…" He sweeps me into an embrace, wrapping his long arms around me, and squeezes me against him. My feet leave the ground as he lifts me, bending his head and bringing his mouth to mine. When he pulls back, my head is spinning.

"You look like an Alpha," I say, running my hands over his broad shoulders, his simple white shirt stretching tight over his muscles. "When did you get so…manly?"

"When I Chose a mate," he says, cocking an eyebrow at me.

"No, I think it just happened recently," I say. "When you took your rightful place in the pack. Now come on, aren't you supposed to dance with me?"

Like last time, we eat, and drink cider, and when the

band assembles on the platform, we dance. The night grows chillier around us, and Harmon holds me close, wrapping his warmth around me. Over his shoulder, I watch the moon. This time, nothing will go wrong.

"What are you thinking about?" Harmon asks, lifting one hand from my waist to smooth his thumb between my eyebrows. "You're frowning."

"I was just thinking about the last time we danced here, during the eclipse, at your coronation."

"Lucky me," he says. "I get to Choose you twice."

I smile at the memory, resting a hand on his strong chest. "Are you sure you didn't think I was Elidi that time?"

"I've known that girl since the day she was born. She couldn't surprise me if she tried."

"How'd I surprise you?"

"The way you kissed me," he murmurs, nuzzling my ear. "I still get shivers when I think about it."

I'm glad only the golden glow of the firelight illuminates my face, and I hope he can't see me blushing. "You're such a flirt," I say lightly.

"Only for you," he says, pulling me against him.

A while later, the music stops. Harmon steps closer to the fire, and one by one, the members of the pack fall silent. Harmon stands straight and tall, his chest out and shoulders back, looking proud and strong and every inch a leader. Looking at him, I must be as proud as he is. He earned this, and he deserves every bit of it.

"As you remember, the last time we did this, it didn't come to a very satisfying conclusion," he says. "Unfortunately, my father is not here to hand the reigns to me, but we will hold the confirmation ceremony tonight in his memory. We will transition and hunt with our brothers and sisters, as always. I am already your Alpha, but the ceremony will be performed by our elders as is tradition. Also, I have already Chosen a mate, but tonight, Stella and I would like to complete our mating ceremony. As your leader, I promised to unite our pack with the neighboring peoples and create peace and unity. Already I am learning these things take time, so please be patient. And remind me of that when I'm not being so patient myself."

A few wolves chuckle.

Harmon smiles. "Some other young wolves are anxious to Choose their mates as well, so let us proceed."

The pack closes in, forming a circle around us. Their eyes sparkle in the firelight, and a chill breeze scatters leaves across the clearing. I shiver, suddenly nervous, but Harmon takes my hands in his, his grip warm and reassuring.

"Stella, you are my mate," he says. "I've known it since the moment you crashed my coronation and tried to pretend you were Elidi. Badly, I might add."

"Hey," I protest, but everyone else is smiling.

Harmon's expression turns serious. "When you walked into the clearing that night, so obviously lost, I knew that you'd found your way there for a reason. I knew in that moment that you were my mate. I admit, it took me by surprise. Instead of dancing with my mate all night, I spent most of the evening avoiding you, mulling over this impossibility. But my wolf knew, and it refused to let me Choose an easier path. This is my destiny. *You* are my destiny."

I can't hold my tongue any longer. "You knew that whole time? And you let me go on making a fool of myself? Thanks a lot."

He shrugs. "Even if I couldn't tell by how different you were, you didn't have the pack bond. I knew you weren't of the Lunessa pack. I'd like to change that tonight. The beginning of an alliance between shifters and wolves. You belong here as much as anyone. You are one of us."

I waited so long to hear those words. Now, my eyes threaten to spill over with tears. "I can't believe you knew all along," I whisper. "And you still picked me."

"As always, my wolf was right. The wolf knows, even when the man does not. I didn't know how it would work, but I knew you were the woman I'd spend the rest of my life loving and protecting. I guess that will have to be good enough."

"It is," I say, and I throw my arms around his neck and pull him down for a kiss. When I break away, the pack moves in closer, joining hands.

"We join this pair by calling upon the Lunessa pack's founding father, Alpha Oberon Shoals, to unite these two souls as mates," they say. "May your union bring happiness, joy, and plenty. May the Goddess Diana bless you with children to increase this pack and prosperity to share with your neighbor. And may you love and nurture each other, this pack, and our land with willing and grateful hearts."

"We will," Harmon says, and I repeat the words. Everyone cheers, and a hundred people seem ready to embrace me and hand me cider.

This time, Harmon says we'll take care of all the business before the eclipse is total, since it's later this time, at nearly two in the morning. A few other wolves Choose mates, and we all cheer for them. They will wait a few full moons before their official mating ceremony.

After that, the wolves all pledge their loyalty to Harmon again, though he says it's not necessary. The others seem to disagree, and the elders say it's better if it is done properly now. "In case anyone has a mind to question your authority again," an elder says, and I know we're all thinking of Yvonne. After the battle, Harmon explained to them what had happened, and they had a funeral for my mother. But sometimes, I still catch someone looking at me a certain way, or I feel someone watching me, but when I look up, I'm alone. Her shadow still lingers, the horror of what Yvonne did. And I still find myself looking around from time to time, wondering if she's still here, mirroring another wolf, biding her time.

When the elders have made the decision that we will do the whole ceremony as if Harmon were taking over for the first time, they join us in our circle around the fire ring, where embers glow softly among the ashes. Harmon stands up and clears his throat. "Brothers and sisters," he says. "I gave you all a choice when I fought the sorceress, to stay with me or leave. Again, now that you've been under my command, I offer you the chance to find another pack if this one does not satisfy you. I will not force you to stay in my pack. I will not order the pack to shun you, and you are welcome to visit or return if you choose. I am releasing you with good will and peacefulness."

Everyone seated around the fire shakes their heads and

murmurs in protest. Harmon stands silent, waiting another second, two, three. Just when I begin to relax, sure that no one will stand up, clothing rustles to my left, drawing my attention. Someone is climbing to her feet. My gasp is drowned by those of the rest of the pack.

"My Alpha," Elidi says, bowing her head. She swallows before going on. "I ask to be released. You are kind to make such an offer, and I know not all Alphas would do so. I am grateful to you, and I hope one day to return and join the pack again. But I've always wanted to see what else is out there, and now is the right time for me."

Harmon looks like he's been punched in the gut. "Ellie," he says, the nickname that is reserved for him alone, that not even Mother or Zora used.

I sit frozen, my head spinning. It shouldn't surprise me, but it does. It stuns me senseless.

Elidi holds up a hand. "You have always been fair to me," she says to Harmon. "It's nothing that you've done wrong. You haven't failed me. It's my own failing, if anything. They say my mother was always rebellious, so maybe I got it from her. Or maybe it's my shifter side. I love this pack, and I hope you will accept me back if I come home. But I need to do this on my own."

"You can't," Zora cries, her dark eyes seeming to spark with firelight as she glares up at her sister.

"I'm sorry," Elidi says. She reaches down to stroke Zora's hair, but Zora shoves her hand away.

"What am I supposed to do?" Zora demands. "Mother's dead, Stella's gone. And now you?"

"You can come home with us," Fernando's father says quietly. "You're my daughter, too."

"Fine," Zora says, crossing her arms over her chest. "Elidi's cooking is so bad she'd probably poison me if I kept living with her, anyway."

"Alpha?" Elidi asks, turning her attention to Harmon. The pack sits frozen, waiting for Harmon's answer.

"I…" He croaks out the word, his eyes flooded with so much betrayal I think he might cry, or tear her to bits. His Adam's apple bobs once, twice, as he swallows. His cheek twitches.

"I will hunt with you tonight," Elidi says quickly. "But I would like you to release me in the morning."

"I will stand by my word," Harmon says stiffly.

"Thank you," she says. "Since I won't be a member of this pack, I'll go home and pack while you finish the coronation ceremony. I'll be back for the hunt." With that, she turns and starts down the dirt trail where, so long ago, she told me this was what she wanted. She has a dream, and I've always known it. I just never thought I'd be the one staying, and she'd be the one leaving.

I want to run after her, grab her shoulders and shake her. I want to ask how she can do this to me, leave when we're just getting to know each other. At last, we are free to do just that—know the sister so much like us that most people couldn't tell us apart. I thought I'd have years to befriend her, to make up for all the lost years when I didn't even know she existed.

But that's selfish. I can't keep her here just so I can have a family, the one thing I've always wanted more than anything in the world. The thing I want so much that all those silly childhood dreams I used to have are washed away by it.

But Elidi doesn't have the same dreams as I do, I remind myself. We may look alike, but we're not identical on the inside. She grew up with a sister. To her, it may not hold the same allure as it does for me. There is something else she wants more than anything. Not to belong—she's always belonged—but to be alone. The one thing I've had way too much of.

For a solid minute after she leaves, no one speaks. Then Zora snorts. "She's crazy if she wants to be a lone wolf. Who's going to protect her from all the dangers out there? Other packs aren't so nice, and humans could find out, and Diana knows what else. And who wants to be alone, anyway? Being alone sucks."

"You know, you can come visit me," I tell her. "Not to hang out. I mean, we have nothing in common. But I am kind of your sister. Just half, not like that counts or anything."

She rolls her eyes. "Whatever. I might, if you'll make me dinner when I come."

"Always the haggler."

Our exchange seems to thaw the group, and we move on. I slip up beside Harmon while the others are gossiping about my sister.

"I need to go talk to her," I say. "Just for a minute."

He leans in and kisses my forehead, then smiles down at me. "Go."

33

The darkness is deep around me as I jog down the path towards Mother's house, but I'm no longer afraid of the trees or the creatures in the woods. The ghosts might snatch me up to give me a message to pass along, or reach out and touch me out of mischievousness or boredom, but they are not malevolent.

When I turn down the path to Mother's house, I can sense and smell its emptiness before I walk in. My heart cramps painfully inside me. I'm too late. She's gone.

I turn and race back up the drive. She said she'd hunt with us. She didn't even tell me goodbye. Not that we're close, but I thought our blood bond meant something even to her. Our twin bond.

Remembering that, I hesitate, send out my energy along that channel. It's not strong, like I can read her mind. But I seem to be able to feel where she is, maybe even sense when she's in danger. That might come in handy when she's a lone wolf. I know Harmon wouldn't hesitate to run to her rescue, whether or not she's officially a member of his pack. She'll always be more than that. Now that we're mated, she's family to him, too.

I race up the steps to our cabin and burst in, throwing open the door. Relief floods through me when I see the figure standing at our window, looking out at the moon.

"You're here," I say, sinking to the couch in relief.

Elidi turns and braces her hands on the windowsill behind her. She's changed into jeans and a hoodie. "I'm sorry I didn't tell you before," she says, looking at her bare feet. "I had to know if he'd let me leave before I made a big announcement."

"I just can't believe you're leaving," I say. "I mean, I can. But I can't."

Elidi scuffs her toe against the rug. "Did he say anything when I left?"

"No."

"Listen, I know this seems sudden, but…"

"Not really," I say. "We tried to escape two years ago."

"There's more," she says. "Come and look." She motions for me to follow her into my bedroom, where she steps up to the mirror. "Show me the faces of all my sisters by blood," she says, staring intently into the mirror. The picture begins to swirl, and chills race up my arms. My face remains where it is, but three other faces form out of the mist beside me—Zora, Astrid, and a girl I've never seen before.

"I think I know when Mother was possessed," Elidi says. "I think it happened a few times before it became permanent. She started getting up at night, saying she couldn't sleep."

I turn away from the mirror, rubbing my arms to warm them. "Because Yvonne could invade her body when she was sleeping."

"One time, she came in my room and woke me up. She asked me to feel through our bond if you were still alive. I told her you were. I'm sorry."

I shrug, wishing I could think of a reason for her to stay. "It doesn't matter."

"After I told her, she told the whole pack. People lost a lot of respect for Harmon when they found out he'd lied about that. Wolves...we don't really lie to each other. Not within our own pack."

"That was my idea," I admit.

"It wasn't a very good one," she says with a little smile, sinking onto the edge of my bed.

I realize now what a huge thing I asked of Harmon, to betray his own pack to keep me safe from my mother. And he did it.

My heart breaks a little knowing that. He was willing to risk losing the respect of the pack, maybe even their loyalty, for me. It's not just that the wolves have to obey him. I didn't understand that for so long, how everyone could want an Alpha ordering them around. But it's more than that. It's trusting him to do what's best for the pack, respecting him enough to let him make decisions, make mistakes, and learn from them.

I'm proud to be one of the Lunessa pack, proud of the leader Harmon will become. Still, I'm damn sure not going to obey him all the time. He let me make my own mistake that time, even took the fall for it. Suddenly, all I want to do is be with him right now. I should be there on our night, on his coronation night, not chasing after a sister who doesn't want to be chased. What if something happens like last time, and I'm not there? I'm sure he'd rather I not be—I can't protect myself, and it would prob-ably put him in further danger to have to fight for me. But

I can't bear the thought of anything happening to him while I'm gone.

"I should get back to him," I say.

"Wait," Elidi says, then rushes ahead with her story. "That's not what I wanted to tell you. After Mother asked that, I didn't understand why Harmon would lie. So I borrowed the mirror from Zora, and I asked to see my sister. It showed me Zora. I guess that's who I think of first when I use that word."

I nod, trying to hide how much that fact stings.

She laughs a little. "So then I asked to see an image of all my sisters by blood. Instead of showing me two, it showed me four." She nods at the mirror, and I glance back at it.

"I know about Astrid. Dad's daughter from…" I swallow, not wanting to say it. "Who's the last one?"

"Yeah, I guess Dad really wasn't cut out to marry a wolf," she says, approaching the mirror to stand beside me.

I open my mouth to defend him—I'm a shifter, too, after all—but close it again. She's right. Not only did he have a wife before my mother, he apparently has illegitimate children running all over these valleys. To be fair, when I was a kid he always said I was the only girl he needed, even when I urged him to date. Though women always flirted with him, and he was the friendly, gregarious type, he never brought anyone home. At least he spared me that, though he was apparently getting around just fine when he went out. Maybe that's what all those late-night meetings were. Not work. Not shifting.

Elidi goes on. "Remember how I said that a few times, we had short truces with the shifters?"

"Yeah…"

"When I was about six, there was a short one right after Fernando lost his arm. We'd go over to the shifter valley to see Dr. Golden all the time, on that same trail over the mountain I showed you."

"Right. She's from here, too."

"For a while she lived there. I didn't like Zora much then. She was my annoying tag-along sister. But Dr. Golden had a daughter I adored. We played together all the time that summer. Then one day Mother had a big fight with Dr. Golden, and we weren't allowed to go over anymore."

She smiles and bites at a hangnail. "Except I went over anyway. Even after the truce was over, for a couple years, we'd sneak up to see each other and play in the woods. Then one day, she started acting really mean. I got mad at her and left, and I never went back. A few years later, we had another truce with them for a few months, and I went over with Mother, but she was gone."

"Because she lived in Oklahoma City," I say. "Dad said that's why we moved there. To be close to Dr. Golden."

"I think it was the other way around, because you already lived there. But I guess there's a reason they wanted to be close." She nods at the mirror. "I had no idea we were related. We were best friends, that's all."

"That explain the big fight Mother and Dr. Golden had."

"Right."

"Except…Dr. Golden never mentioned a daughter," I say. "I used to tease Dad about her, telling him they should get married so I could have a mom. And she came over for cookouts and stuff. They were friends, she and Dad. I don't think she'd keep his daughter from him."

"When she came back to the Three Valleys last year, I asked her about Violet," she says. "She said Violet went missing that winter after we stopped hanging out. They never found her. That was part of why she moved away—it happened here. But I can find her. With the mirror." Her eyes glow with anticipation.

I hesitate, wanting to be selfish, to hold onto it. Not because it's beautiful, but because I can find Elidi with the mirror. If something happens to her, if she's in danger, will my twin bond be enough? With the mirror, I could see if she was okay.

But I know I'm being unfair. It's just a thing, an object. Last time I held onto an object, I was so wrapped up in having something of my own that I didn't even notice that the woman who gave it to me wasn't my mother. "Okay."

Elidi's eyes widen. "Really? I can have it?"

"I don't know how you'll carry it."

"I don't have to," she says, turning it over. "The mirror isn't magical. There's a seeing stone buried in this wood. That's why you can see." She pulls a pocketknife from her pocket and starts gouging the wood. A cry of protest rises to my lips, but I hold it back. If she wants to find her best friend, our other sister, I can't blame her. I want my family together, too.

At last, Elidi finds it. She digs her knife deep into the wood and splinters it. A white, iridescent stone, about the size of a marble but elongated and flattened a bit, slides out like an egg. "A seeing stone," she says in awe, picking it up and holding it cupped in her palms. "I've heard of these, but I didn't know we had one all these years until your friend Kale told me what they did. Apparently, they're priceless treasures to the faeries. There's only a couple in the whole world."

"Won't that make it dangerous for you to carry it around?"

"I'll be careful," she says with a shrug, all reverence gone the moment she snaps her fingers closed around the stone and can't see it. She slips it into her pocket and flips her knife closed. "And when I find our sister, I'll come back. I promise. The four of us will be together for the first time, like a family." A tiny smile begins to form on her lips, and I can feel the excitement radiating from her. "I always wanted a bigger family. I always hoped Fernando and his dad would come live with us. And now I have you, and Zora, and Dad's two kids..."

I start to point out she'll be alone, not with all of us. That she's leaving all she has on the chance she'll find some friend she had for a few years when she was a kid, and who knows if the girl will even remember her or want to come back here. But I decide to be happy for her instead. "Are you sure you don't just want to get out of here so no one can tell you what to do?" I tease.

A grin splits her face, and she bites it back, as if slightly ashamed of how happy she is to be leaving. "After living with Mother for seventeen years, can you blame me?"

"Not even a little."

34

When I get back to the fire, Harmon slips an arm around my waist and squeezes me against him. "I was worried about you," he whispers into my hair. "What took you so long?"

"I'll explain later," I tell him. "Right now, it's time for you."

The elders come up and Harmon is sworn in. The confirmation is complete. Harmon is Alpha. We make a circle around the fire. The moon is just a bright slice, a crescent of silver hugging the edge of the growing red orb.

Just as we take our positions around the fire, a branch snaps in the woods. The wolves freeze, their nostrils flaring. "Not this again," Fernando's father growls as fallen leaves rustle and crunch under approaching footsteps. Two of the other men strip off their clothes and begin to shift.

I wait, my heart hammering, images from the last eclipse flashing through my mind with dizzying speed. A man who stepped out of the woods holding a lantern. A girl with red hair he threw at Harmon's feet. Animals of all shapes and sizes emerging from the dark forest, tearing into the wolves. My mother's scream of pure fury—I swallow hard, realizing now that she was going for that lantern. The one that contained Yvonne. If she'd killed her then, Yvonne wouldn't have come back. I'm the one who saved her.

In return, she killed my mother.

But if my mother had just told me, had only explained everything to me then, I would have known better. Her secrets cost her life.

At last, a figure pops out of the woods, stumbling forward and tripping on a long dress. Another flash of *déjà vous* sweeps over me. But this is a different girl, one with pale auburn hair falling loose from the braid that circles her head like a crown. She is, after all, the shifter queen. But right now, she looks like a flustered mess.

Astrid straightens and smooths down her hair with both hands as if just realizing she has an audience. But before she can open her mouth to speak, I launch myself at her. She won't get away this time. This time, the shifters didn't send a big scary bodyguard with their offering. She's just a small girl with scratches on her cheeks and twigs in her hair. And I can take her, even in human form.

I slam into her, knocking her flat on her back. She won't get away this time.

"Wait," she cries. "Don't kill me!"

She begins to scramble away, but I grab her and slam her onto her back, leaping onto her. With a shriek, she begins to shift. But before she can disappear into thin air like she did before, I straddle her narrow hips and grip her throat with one hand.

"If you shift, I'll snap your neck like the chicken you are," I snarl at her, not sure if she knows I'm nowhere near strong enough to do that.

"I won't shift," she says quickly, going still under me,

her body going solid and fully human again. "Just please let me go."

"You're the one who showed up uninvited," I remind her. "What do you want?"

"I need help," she says, her eyes flitting from one corner to the other.

I grab a rock off the ground and pull my hand back, clutching it in my fist. "No one here is going to help you," I growl. "Give me my shifting back, and I'll think about letting you live."

"Okay," she says, gripping my wrist, trying to pry my hand from her throat. "I'll undo it. Please, just don't put me in your dungeon."

I narrow my eyes at her. "Undo the spell. Now."

She closes her eyes and takes a shaky breath, then whispers a chant. Inside, my tiger stirs, then roars angrily to get out. I let her.

In seconds, I am not a girl in a white dress but a white tiger, outweighing this twig by hundreds of pounds. Keeping my paw on her chest, I stand over her, barely feeling her thin fingers digging into my fur.

I open my mouth and let out a roar in her face, one so powerful it sends a burst of wind up the surrounding mountains, rippling the leaves on the ghostly trees that fill our valley.

"Please," Astrid begs, her whole body shaking. Tears fill her eyes, and I see how helpless she is. She's pathetic now, helpless to stop me. That's why she trapped me, just like my parents did. My whole life, I've lived in the confines of my human body, unable to be my whole self. Of all the people who made that happen, she is the only one left. My mother, my father, and her mother are all gone. There's one person left to kill.

I remember Harmon's flat statement about what must be done. He had to kill Yvonne, because she had taken my mother's place and was trying to take his. That was his fight. This is mine.

I open my mouth to rip out Astrid's heart, but my teeth sink into only fabric. She did it again. Enraged, I roar out my fury. But then I see something moving inside her dress. Just as a bird explodes from it, I leap forward, snapping her into my mouth. Her wings thrash uselessly against my jaws, her body clamped inside my mouth. Feathers struggle against my tongue. In that moment, I look up, and I see all the wolves watching. Waiting for me to dispense with this so they can get on with the hunt.

No one would blame me. No one would think twice. This is what they would do. Kill the intruder and go about their business. We're animals. It's our nature.

And yet…I wasn't raised an animal. I was raised a human, and though it wasn't by choice, I can't shed that nature as easily as they can. But I can choose to shed it. I remember Harmon standing on my mother's lawn the first day I shifted, telling me I had a choice.

I can embrace my animal and kill my tormentor, as an animal would do. Or I can stay forever more allied with my human side, and show mercy, a trait that belongs to humans. And I've been human too long.

My teeth tighten, and Astrid goes still in my mouth.

The wolves are all waiting.

But then I remember something else Harmon said. I'm an animal. But I'm also a human. And I know that right here on my tongue is the one thing I've always wanted, no matter how far it is from what I pictured when I prayed for a family.

I drop Astrid's body on the ground at my feet, a lump covered in wet feathers. My heart lurches as I roll her over, sure that she's dead. Suddenly, I don't feel quite so powerful. I feel like a bully, like my mother when she slapped me as I cowered in her attic. And I understand then why the wolves never intervened. It was her duty to protect the pack from outsiders, and she did. Just as quickly as it came, my anger dissipates, replaced by shame. My tiger slinks away, sulking, as I shift back to human. I send her a quick promise to let her out often now that I can.

"Astrid?" I say, holding the raven in my hands.

Suddenly, she shrinks in my hands. But I hold them tight on her, until I can only feel a tiny lump between my palms.

I sigh. "Shift back to human so we can talk. I won't hurt you if you don't cast more spells."

After a long moment, the seed-like bug between my hands swells, and I scoot back as she smoothly slides into human form.

"Are you done shifting?" I ask, grasping her neck in case she pulls any more tricks.

She nods, tears pooling in her eyes.

"Why are you here?" Harmon asks from behind me.

"I need help," Astrid says, sitting up and wrapping her arms around her naked form.

"Why would we help you after what you did to me?" I ask, pushing her back again.

"My mother made me do that. I'll—I'll tell you where she is if you let me go. I'll do anything."

My eyes narrow. "Where is she?"

Astrid points a shaky finger to the edge of the clearing and sniffs. "She's in that tree."

"How do you know?"

She sniffs again, wiping the tears off her cheek. "Because I put her there."

Slipping off her, I gather the tatters of my dress around me. Apparently, it wasn't designed to fit both a human and a Siberian tiger. I'll have to work on that. Maybe take that up instead of being a model—a fashion designer who makes cute clothes that work for both humans and animals.

"Why would you do that?" I ask.

"Because she locked me in that lighthouse my whole life," she says, sitting up and scooting back, dragging her pretty dress in the dirt. Apparently, she's more concerned about her proximity to me than salvaging her dress.

"Oh, kind of like you locked my tiger inside me?" I snarl.

"Yes," she whispers. "I'm sorry. And I'm sorry if I interrupted the pack meeting. I just thought this would be a good time to talk to you, when you're assigning roles. I didn't come to fight. I didn't even bring backup. And see, I even wore a dress." She holds up a pinch of fabric, a hopeful smile on her face.

"What do you want our help with?" Something about her is so naïve, so childlike, I can't help but pity her.

"I need help with…everything," she says, gulping. "I don't know how to be a queen. My mother always said she'd help me, but what she really meant was that she'd do it for me. And then you had to go and try to kill her, and if I hadn't locked her in that tree, she'd have killed one of you. And now I don't know what I'm doing."

She breaks off and covers her face, choking back a sob. "The shifters are terrible. They laugh in my face when I tell them I'm their leader. How do you get your people to gather like this, so orderly? And forget listening. They all think I'm a joke, and half of them won't leave their trailers because they're afraid their meth labs will explode while they're gone. I hate them!" She breaks off again, takes a ragged breath, and bursts into tears.

I glance up at Harmon for help, but he is only watching soberly, with the rest of the wolves. He nods towards her, his face serious. He's trusting me to solve this, or maybe curious what role I want to play in shifter politics. My place here is established. I'm half wolf by blood. But I'm also a shifter princess. The possibilities race through my mind. If I was the shifter queen, we'd have an immediate alliance between the pack and the shifters. Or at least their leaders.

I turn back to Astrid. "So you don't want to be queen? You want me to do it for you."

"Would you?" she asks, grabbing desperately at my arm, her fear forgotten.

"No," I say, pulling away. "That sounds horrible. They'd laugh at me, too."

"But you're a tiger," she wails. "I'm a bird. And you're just as much the heir as I was. Let me do this as my duty to the shifter people. My first act as queen will be to turn over the throne to you."

"Why don't you use your magic? You're half witch, right?"

She sniffs. "I'm not that powerful. I'm not even a real witch, because I wasn't born with magic. She gave me magic to do whatever she needed me to do. Otherwise, I'm just a shifter. I can cast a few spells I learned from Mother Dear. But that's it."

"Powerful enough to take away their shifting," I say. "That would get their attention."

"They'd kill me." She wipes her face, casting her eyes at the dirt. "I thought you might help. She always said you'd fight to be queen, and here I am giving it to you, and you don't want it. I should have known she was lying. I'm sorry. I shouldn't have come."

"I could try..." I say slowly.

"Really?" Her eyes are so hopeful, so scared to hope, it makes my stomach turn. She's the furthest thing from queenly right now, with her splotchy face, red eyes, and dirt-streaked body. Again, that hopeful smile trembles on her lips like a question. Now I know why she looks familiar—the cupid's bow lips, her blue-gray eyes. If I look just like my mother, well, she looks like Dad.

I hold up a hand. "I could try to help—if you agree to a treaty between the shifters and wolves. I need to be able to come and go between here and there without any danger to myself or anyone else. And we need hunting land now that one of our mountainsides is gone. It could take years to recover. I need the truce to last. Not just until you figure out how to be their queen. We should have a good relationship with all the valleys. We need to protect ourselves from outsiders, and it would be a lot easier if we all helped each other."

She nods like a bobblehead the entire time I speak. "Agreed," she says, standing and brushing her dirty hands together. "I'll sign whatever papers, and get my people to sign...our people. Well, actually, you might have to do that part."

"Are you sure you want to do this?" I ask, squinting up at her. "Bringing me in to help isn't going to earn you any respect in their eyes."

"But you're equally the heir as much as I am. You can be my co-queen."

After a pause, I stand and hold out my hand for her to shake. "Okay. If you'll be my sister."

35

While I was busy with Astrid, I forgot to watch the moon. When I look up, the wolves are all waiting, looking supremely uncomfortable. And then I see the moon, a huge red orb in the sky, earth's shadow blocking it from reflecting the sun. The wolves are past due for shifting, but they were waiting for me.

"I'm sorry," I mutter.

"Are you kidding?" Harmon asks, grabbing me and pulling me in for a rough kiss. "You were brilliant. You were…" For a second, his eyes flicker out, glazing with the effort of holding back his wolf. Now that I've done it, I know how hard it is to control.

"Let's talk later," I say.

"Thank you," he says quietly. "And thank you for… negotiating so brilliantly for us."

"For *us*," I say, squeezing his hand.

His gaze sizzles with heat as it meets mine, his animal wanting to come out. The promise in his eyes that makes my cheeks warm.

But for now, I have to share him. He raises his voice to carry over the others. "Let's hunt."

A raucous, wild cheer goes up. Clothes are shredded in the wolves' hurry to undress.

"What about me and Astrid?" I ask, knowing we should be gone, not witnessing this sacred ritual.

"Stay," he says. "Hunt with me. You're my mate."

"Should I try to shift into a wolf?"

He shakes his head. "You're not a wolf, and I'm not asking you to be one. Be yourself."

"Can I come, too?" Astrid asks.

Harmon's cheek twitches, and I know he's measuring the cost of this. Will the other wolves disagree? But he's the Alpha, and he doesn't allow more than that one second of indecision. "Yes," he says. "As a show of our faith in the shifters' new leader, and the unity of our peoples."

"Cool," Astrid says, hopping up and standing before him, completely naked, with no shame.

My jealous streak flares, and my tiger roars to come out. While Harmon drops to all fours to shift, I try to catch Astrid's eye with my glare, but she doesn't notice.

"What should I shift into?" she asks innocently, still standing there stark naked.

That's it. I let my tiger out, and she leaps forward at Astrid, sensing a threat. Astrid shrieks and shifts into an owl, and I wonder if she was the owl I saw watching me a long time ago when I tried to escape. My tiger doesn't care. Her first instinct is to kill, to ask questions...well, never. But I reign her in, getting the hang of being in her skin again. Once, I might have let her swipe at Astrid. Hell, I did try to eat her five minutes ago. But now, I control that tiger instinct even as I race along the trail beneath a pair of outstretched wings. Astrid is my ally now. My sister.

＊　＊　＊

Ahead, the howl of wolves echoes up the mountainsides, through our valley. One day, it will echo through all of the Three Valleys. I can feel it. With Harmon's determination and leadership, with my ties to the shifters, it will happen. We will make it happen.

I race to catch up, the pads of my huge feet gripping the ground, my claws gripping boulders as we start up the mountain. A little white wolf slips in beside me, and a brown one takes my other side, throwing her shoulder against my leg as I stride forward. I stumble, and she prances around, her tongue hanging out, laughter in her eyes. I swipe at her with one paw, but she turns and streaks up the mountain. My tiger wants to lie down and preen, reveling unashamedly in the swelling joy in my heart.

But she catches a scent, and her attention turns. I let her carry me, let her take over. A hunger fills me, not my stomach but my soul. And I love it. For the moment, everything is right in the world. We pass a wolf, then two more. Outpacing everyone, until we're running shoulder to shoulder with Harmon. Pride swells inside me. I'm no longer the scared little outcast hidden away in an attic. I fought my way up, and now I'm the strongest one here. I'm at the front of the pack, next to my Alpha.

This is where I belong.

This is me. Girl. Tiger. Queen.

The End

Also by Lena Mae Hill

Young Witch Series

(companion series to *Girl Among Wolves*)

Twisted

Caged (2019)

Winslow Witch Chronicles

(prequel series to *Young Witch Series)*

Magic of the Void

Sister of the Sea

Hosting Gods Series

Emerge

Ignite

Ascend

The Superiors Series

Blood Moon

Blood Thirst

Blood Oath

Blood Sport

Blood Lust (2018)

Blood Night (short story)

Lena
Mae Hill

Hey, y'all!

I'm a southern author of fiction of many flavors. I was born and raised in Arkansas and make my home there today, along with my family, a cat, two dogs, and eleven chickens.

I've been writing in one form or another all my life. I adore fairytales, especially the way they portray the dark and twisted parts of human nature. Those original tales inspired this series. To read about the witches who appear throughout Stella's story, check out the *Young Witch* series.

My related prequel stories, the *Winslow Witch Chronicles* may also appeal to you. Check out these and more by searching for my name on Amazon. And don't forget to leave a review!

www.ingramcontent.com/pod-product-compliance
Lightning Source LLC
Chambersburg PA
CBHW030111260626
47156CB00008B/2615